THE SECRET OF DEVIL'S CANYON

When Mayor Maxwell and his daughter are brutally murdered, feelings in Bear Creek run high. And when the killer is caught and sentenced to life in prison, the townsfolk demand a lynching. So Sheriff Bryce calls in Nathaniel McBain to spirit the killer away through Devil's Canyon to Beaver Ridge jail. Nathaniel, just one step ahead of the pursuing mob, loses ground, then realizes that he's facing an even bigger problem: his prisoner may be innocent after all . . .

I. J. PARNHAM

THE SECRET OF DEVIL'S CANYON

Complete and Unabridged

LINFORD
Leicester

First published in Great Britain in 2011 by
Robert Hale Limited
London

First Linford Edition
published 2012
by arrangement with
Robert Hale Limited
London

The moral right of the author has been asserted

British Library CIP Data

Parnham, I. J.
    The secret of Devil's Canyon. - -
(Linford western library)
1. Western stories.
2. Large type books.
I. Title II. Series
823.9′2–dc23

ISBN 978–1–4448–1276–3

Published by
F. A. Thorpe (Publishing)
Anstey, Leicestershire

Set by Words & Graphics Ltd.
Anstey, Leicestershire
Printed and bound in Great Britain by
T. J. International Ltd., Padstow, Cornwall

This book is printed on acid-free paper

Prologue

'I'm going with Seymour, after all,' Cooper Metcalf said.

'Why the hurry?' Cooper's boss Washington Cody said, while hunched over his anvil. 'You still have work to do today.'

'But he's paying me just to take him up into Devil's Canyon.'

'Then go.' Washington waved a dismissive hand at him. 'I'll look after things here, as always. Just don't expect that your job will still be waiting for you when you get back.'

Cooper shrugged and hurried off to gather up his belongings while Washington made himself busy in his workshop. In truth he had no work to do, so the money Cooper would earn would mean he wouldn't have to feel guilty about not paying him a full wage this week.

That didn't mean he couldn't make a

1

point about Cooper's ability to be elsewhere whenever there was work to be done.

'I'll be gone for a week,' Cooper said when he returned to the workshop with a saddlebag over his shoulder.

'And you're just going up to my old house?'

'At first. That's where I found the map, but where that'll lead us to, Seymour doesn't know yet. I guess that's why he wants a guide.'

The two men stood in silence for a while until Washington gave a brief nod, then held a hand to the side, signifying that Cooper should go. He joined Cooper in walking to the door where he waited until Cooper was about to move off before he mentioned the one matter that he'd wanted to discuss for the last week.

'What should I tell Narcissa, if she comes looking for you?'

Cooper laughed and turned to face him. 'Now that would be a surprise. The last thing she said to me was that

2

if I came within fifty yards of her again her father would run me out of town.'

Washington joined Cooper in laughing. 'In that case, if she does come, I'll tell her you're sorry.'

'About what?'

'I don't know. But it can't do no harm.' Washington kicked at the ground. 'Go on. Enjoy yourself and come back in a better mood than you've been in for the last week.'

Cooper nodded, clearly pleased to get his approval, then headed off sporting the first cheery smile Washington had seen him produce since his unfortunate argument with Narcissa. Presently the rattling of a wagon drawing away sounded. Then, with there being nothing useful he could do this afternoon, Washington closed up the workshop and made his way round to the adjoining house.

He stood on the porch enjoying the high sun and the sound of water rushing by in the nearby Bear Creek, which emerged from Devil's Canyon before carrying on to the town of Bear Creek. With that town now prospering, his was the only building left occupied at the formerly thriving Wilson's Crossing, but enough travellers made their way around the canyon to provide Washington with a frugal living.

A distant screech sounded.

Washington strained his hearing, searching for the source of the noise while trying to work out what it had been. It hadn't sounded like any animal he'd ever heard, nor had it sounded like a person attempting an animal cry.

He collected his Winchester and headed off towards the creek. On the way he listened for further sounds, but he heard nothing. He didn't think it could have been Cooper, as he should be at least a mile into the canyon by now.

He looked that way. Silhouetted against the sky a group of riders was heading towards the canyon. They were a half-mile away and they appeared for only a few seconds before the undulating terrain took them from view, but Washington reckoned there were four men.

A rustling sounded in the scrub beside him.

With pensive slow paces Washington moved towards the sound. It had come from twenty yards away and he craned his neck, but he could see nothing moving ahead, although when he reached the spot the scrub had been flattened, as if someone had been lying there.

He knelt and saw faint tracks on the hard ground and the broken stems that suggested someone had crawled, or perhaps been dragged, away. His gaze rose and alighted on a darker form which, when he moved closer, proved to be a man lying on his chest.

Now what are you doing here? Washington said to himself as he hurried to the man's side. But the moment he turned the man over he got his answer.

Washington jerked back in horror, bile rising in his throat. He took deep breaths to calm himself. When he'd gathered his composure he reached out to check for signs of life, but then thought better of it. The man's head had rocked back to display a throat that had been cut so savagely that bone was visible amidst the raw muscle.

Washington's shock heightened when he slipped around the body and got a full view of the face. It was Mayor Maxwell.

This man had come out to Wilson's Crossing only once before, to warn Cooper to stay away from his daughter Narcissa. What he was doing here this time Washington didn't know but, whatever the reason, he had to go to Bear Creek to fetch Sheriff Bryce.

He turned on his heel and walked straight into the chest of Bryce's deputy, Chuck Albright.

'What are you doing?' Albright muttered, peering past Washington at the body.

'It's the mayor,' Washington babbled. 'Someone's killed him.'

'Someone has.' Albright drew his six-shooter and thrust it up under Washington's chin. 'But luckily I know who did it.'

1

The man was running so fast he looked as if he were trying to save a life. The straggling line of baying men at his heels suggested it was his own.

Nathaniel McBain stopped on the boardwalk outside a mercantile to watch him approach. He was already late for his appointment with Sheriff Bryce, but the pursuing mob took the question of whether he should intervene out of his hands when the nearest chaser threw himself at the fleeing man. He caught him around the waist and his momentum sent both men skidding to the ground.

The quarry jerked an elbow back into the pursuer's face, knocking him away. Then he scrambled to his feet, but the man grabbed a trailing ankle and held on. That ended the pursuit. Within seconds the eager mob surrounded

8

their quarry and cut off his escape routes.

The man got to his feet. Like a trapped animal he darted from side to side, seeking a way out, but every time he moved for an opening at least two men closed ranks and pushed him back into the circle.

Then they moved in.

Nathaniel paced on to the hardpan and joined one of the few people here whom he recognized: James Douglas, the owner of the Golden Star. James was standing outside the circle, the press of people effectively relegating him to an onlooker.

'What's this about?' Nathaniel asked.

'Cooper Metcalf escaped from the jailhouse,' James said while rocking from foot to foot seeking to get a better view of what was happening within the circle. 'But we Bear Creek folk like our justice.'

Nathaniel considered pressing for more details, but James's comment suggested that whatever had happened

9

was common knowledge and he could get the details later. As James sought an opening in the brawl, he turned away to head down the road to the law office.

He slipped past the circle just as Cooper hurled himself at a gap that had formed between two men, seeking to break free. He'd picked two of the smaller men and he knocked them over. Then he moved to run, but he covered only a few paces before the circle re-formed around him.

He was pushed over, held down, and then the beating started. Kicks and stamps rained down on him as everyone sought a spare bit of flesh on which they could take out their anger.

From amongst the forest of swirling arms and legs, Cooper clawed his head and shoulders out. He looked along the road, drinking in the sight of a freedom that was beyond him. His gaze moved round to look at Nathaniel.

They locked gazes. Nathaniel reckoned he had seen Cooper before during his regular trips to Bear Creek, and maybe Cooper recognized him, or maybe he just noticed that Nathaniel was the only one not looking to pummel him. Either way he thrust out an imploring hand from under the press of bodies.

'Help me,' he murmured. Then he disappeared beneath a stamping heap of humanity.

Aside from Nathaniel, only two other men hadn't joined in, and they'd been approaching at a more sedate pace. One of the men was playing out a length of rope, making a knot that as he came closer Nathaniel could see would form a noose.

That sight decided it for him.

Nathaniel drew his Peacemaker, thrust it high, and fired. The jumble of men froze. In the silence Nathaniel spoke up.

'Get off him,' he said. 'I'm taking Cooper to Sheriff Bryce.'

A dozen heads turned to him with most of them cast at odd angles. James peeled away to face him.

'Nathaniel,' he said, 'this has nothing to do with you. Stay back.'

'You're right. This has nothing to do with me.' Nathaniel waited until James smiled, then firmed his own expression to a scowl. 'But I'm not standing by while you lynch him.'

He cast his measured gaze across the gathering and for long moments nobody moved. Then James slid off the pile that was holding the captive down and that move initiated a change of heart. One by one men moved aside to leave the captive lying flattened and bruised on the ground.

'You'd have saved yourself a whole heap of trouble,' James said, 'if you'd have listened to me.'

'Are you threatening me?'

James snorted and gave Nathaniel an odd look, as if that hadn't been his meaning. Then he gestured to two men to drag the fallen man to his feet. Even when he was standing, Cooper slumped in their grasp.

They moved off to the law office with

the two men dragging Cooper along and with Nathaniel bringing up the rear. The crowd dispersed although some followed on behind, muttering amongst themselves. The two men who had been bringing a rope melted into the town.

Nobody said anything until they reach the law office. Nathaniel opened the door to find Sheriff Bryce and Deputy Albright studying a map of the town while engaging in animated conversation.

'Not got the time to deal with you right now, Nathaniel,' Bryce said, casting him a brief glance.

'I know. You have an escaped prisoner to find.' Nathaniel stepped aside to let the procession drag Cooper through the door. 'Except we've saved you the trouble. These good citizens tracked him down.'

'Now that sure is a welcome surprise,' Bryce said, tipping back his hat while Albright scowled, then hurried off to take custody of Cooper. 'I was beginning to wonder if I'd ever see him again.'

'He's secure now. So when you're ready, we'll discuss business.'

'We will, and you'll enjoy this task,' Bryce said with a wide smile. 'Cooper is the man you're here to deal with.'

★ ★ ★

Jim was trapped.

Riders were closing in behind and a large uncovered wagon was splayed lengthways across the trail.

Jim Dragon still shook the reins and urged the horses to slip off the trail and take his wagon around the blocked-off route. But then he saw that Pierre Dulaine had chosen a good place to ambush him.

The land sloped upwards to the right at an angle that was steep enough to topple his wagon over. To the left rough rocks poked up amidst the scrub, promising a broken wheel if he tried to pass over them.

Jim drew back on the reins, bringing his sweat-slicked mounts to a halt five yards away from the wagon. His trusty Peacemaker was at his hip, but the three drawn six-shooters trained on him from the back of the wagon said he'd be dead before he'd laid a hand on it.

He glanced over his shoulder to watch the chasing riders spread out around him. When they'd surrounded him, the lead man Pierre Dulaine moved his mount on to draw alongside the seat.

'You gave us quite a chase there, Monsieur Dragon,' he said. There was approval in his tone, but only because that pursuit had ended in his victory.

Jim tipped his hat with the hint of a mocking smile tugging at the corners of his mouth.

'I'm pleased you enjoyed it.' He gestured ahead. 'Now, if you'd be so good as to get this wagon moved aside, I can be on my way.'

Several men laughed. Pierre let the amusement run its course before offering a mocking smile of his own.

'We will move aside . . . ' He raised himself in the saddle to consider the four crates filling the back of Jim's wagon. 'But only after we've removed the burden that was slowing you down.'

Jim cast a rueful glance at the crates, acknowledging the irony of Pierre's comment. Without the weight holding him back, he might have escaped the trap Pierre had set, but then again, the weight was the only reason Pierre was chasing him.

Two men dismounted and headed round to the back of his wagon. They let down the backboard, then clambered up where they quickly found out just how heavy the crates were. Despite straining with a man on both ends, the crates remained firmly in place as if glued to the base of the wagon.

They prised off the top of one crate and looked inside at the tangle of bones before replacing the lid.

'If the haul's too big for you,' Jim said, dragging some entertainment out of the unfortunate situation, 'perhaps you should leave it.'

'The bigger the haul,' Pierre said, 'the bigger the profit.'

'For you.'

'You get the reward of knowing these bones will go to someone who cares, and who is prepared to pay a good price.' Pierre directed two more men to help move the crates. This time they managed to drag them along the wagon floor. 'And what have you found this time?'

Jim shrugged. 'Bones, big bones. I was told they're from dragons who lived long before we were born.'

'Fascinating,' Pierre said in a flat tone that suggested the opposite. 'And that would be the reason why Monsieur Dragon searched for these particular bones?'

'It is,' Jim said as the other wagon with the fresh mounts was moved round to the back of his to speed up the transfer of the crates.

Despite Pierre's scowl that said he

was only making conversation to rub in his victory, he went on to relate the true story, mostly, of how he'd gained his interest in the bones of long-dead reptiles.

As a child his mother had told him his name harked back to the days when giant fire-breathing lizards flew through the skies. He'd been intrigued, but for the next twenty years growing up and then earning a living occupied his time and he'd forgotten about it, until one day an overheard tale in a saloon caught his attention.

A dragon's body had been dug up, a liquor-soaked man reported. It was clearly a tall tale to entertain the whiskey-addled customers, but Jim decided to check it out. It took him a week to find the body and the sight was a disappointment, turning out to be scattered stone objects that barely looked like bones, never mind a dragon.

But six months later, another chance meeting informed him that people would pay for such bones. Jim's wandering life became focused; a childhood interest, a knack for exploring, and a love for the dollar could all be fulfilled if he found more dragons.

Over the years he couldn't help but learn from the people who paid him, and although he now knew the bones weren't those of dragons, he still liked to think they were.

'Even so,' he said, finishing his tale, 'I do know what's really in those crates.'

Pierre shrugged. 'Although I've enjoyed watching you try to distract me while your hand moves closer to your holster, move it one inch nearer and you'll be on the receiving end of a different kind of hot fire.'

As Pierre chuckled at his wit, Jim raised his hands into full view. With an air of resignation he leaned back on his seat and waited for them to unload the four crates. When the wagon now laden down with his hard work had drawn alongside, he considered Pierre.

'Have you finished with me now?' he asked.

Pierre moved his horse closer to look into the back of the now empty wagon. He ran his gaze into the four corners, then on to Jim, as if somehow he might have hidden one of the giant bones about his person. His gaze stuck on the shark's tooth he wore around his neck.

'The tooth,' he said, holding out a hand.

'But that's my lucky tooth.'

'Your *lucky* tooth?' Pierre chuckled. 'Well, who am I to take your lucky tooth? I hope it gives you more luck in finding bones, and then me more dollars when I steal them.'

While still laughing Pierre tipped his hat then waved for the riders to move on out.

Jim watched Pierre leave. When he'd disappeared from view he slipped the string loop holding his lucky tooth over his head and stepped into the back of the wagon.

He knelt in the far corner and inserted the tooth into a knothole, then prised the plank up. A second, false bottom of the wagon came into view.

The long and valuable bones he'd secured there were undamaged. The bones he had put in the crates were the more common, and the less valuable, ones that he'd dug up. Some were just rocks.

Smiling, Jim stepped back on to the seat and, with his lighter load, when he moved off he did so with good speed and with a merry tune on his lips.

2

'So,' Shackleton Frost said when Nathaniel McBain joined him at the bar, 'what's the deal this time?'

Nathaniel merely frowned, letting Sheriff Bryce speak.

'You're to escort Cooper Metcalf to Beaver Ridge jail,' he said when everyone had a drink in front of them. 'But it'll be a tricky mission.'

'We've always delivered the tricky ones to justice,' Shackleton said. 'How many years did this one get?'

'I don't know yet. His trial's tomorrow.'

Both men murmured their surprise at this revelation.

'You must be pretty sure of a conviction to call us in before he even gets sent to jail.'

'I'm not, but if he is found guilty, you'll need to act quickly. He was

Washington Cody's accomplice.'

'Ah,' Shackleton and Nathaniel said together.

Two weeks ago they'd taken Washington Cody to jail for killing Mayor Maxwell, but Bryce had suspected that an accomplice was still at large. Worse, the mayor's daughter had gone missing.

'Narcissa's body hasn't turned up yet, but I found signs of a struggle and plenty of blood. Cooper and her had been seen arguing, so it looks bad for Cooper. Last week I finally tracked him down skulking in Devil's Canyon.' Bryce sighed and gulped his whiskey. 'The murder of a popular young woman has upset a lot of people.'

'Understood. You expecting trouble from any particular quarter?'

Bryce glanced at Nathaniel and raised his eyebrows, inviting him to talk, so he explained about the near lynching he'd stopped earlier.

'After so nearly getting to lynch him, everyone's eager to try again,' Bryce said when he'd finished. 'So when the trial's over, you'll be in the jailhouse and ready to spirit him away before anybody has the time to plan any summary justice.'

Both men nodded and then, with two customers coming to the bar for drinks, Bryce reverted to general chatter, ensuring nobody overheard their plans. Not that he needed to provide much detail. In the year that Nathaniel had worked for Shackleton, they had carried out this routine several times.

Their job was to transport convicted men from the various towns within a few days' ride of Beaver Ridge jail. In that year they'd never lost a prisoner, a record that Shackleton was proud of, but Nathaniel had an especial reason to welcome that record and so, when the customers had left the bar, he brought up the subject.

Accordingly, Bryce drew him down the bar and away from Shackleton even though Nathaniel would tell his colleague everything later.

'Has Judge Matthews mentioned my

situation?' Nathaniel asked.

'He has,' Bryce said. 'You've delighted him, and me too.'

Nathaniel breathed a sigh of relief. A year ago he'd faced a prison sentence for a crime he hadn't committed, but in which he'd had the bad luck to be in the wrong place at the wrong time. He'd been given a chance to avoid jail by taking on a job that nobody had wanted. If he worked without mishap for a year and a day delivering prisoners to the jail, he would be a free man.

Nathaniel had enjoyed working for Shackleton, so he still intended to carry on helping him after completing his term. Shackleton had reckoned he would have no trouble when he came before the judge to review his year's work, but that didn't stop him worrying about it.

'I've just done my job,' Nathaniel said.

'And done it well.' Bryce looked around to check nobody was close. 'But this time you need to be careful.

Cooper was devious enough to get past Deputy Albright and escape.'

'How?'

Bryce winced. 'He somehow got hold of the key to his cell. Then Albright went to sleep. When he awoke . . . '

'I don't make mistakes like that,' Nathaniel said cautiously, sensing the finish before it came.

'You don't, so get him to jail and Governor Bradbury will recommend to Judge Matthews that you have repaid your debt. Fail and . . . '

Bryce left the rest of the statement uncompleted other than with a stern look.

★ ★ ★

'Get your dirty hands off me!'

As the demand had come from a woman, Jim Dragon turned from the bar; when he saw that the woman was clearly not a saloon girl he watched the developing situation with interest.

She was dressed for travel with

trousers and an oversized man's jacket, and her dirt-streaked and flustered face suggested she'd just completed a long journey. The two men blocking her way were as intrigued by her arrival in the saloon as Jim was.

'Now why should I do that?' one man said, ushering her to join him at the bar. 'I just want to buy you a drink and to spend some time with a pretty woman.'

'I don't want to spend time with you,' she snapped, digging in her heels, but failing to stop him pulling her closer. 'I'm looking for a man.'

The two men hooted with laughter.

'Then you've come to the right place,' the second man said.

She looked them both up and down with disdain.

'I don't think so.'

This comment only made the men laugh all the harder.

'I like a woman with spirit,' the second man said, taking her other arm. 'Now, what do you want this man to do to you?'

She pouted, snorting her breath through her nostrils as she appeared to search for the right withering response, but the men did at least release her and stand back to enjoy her predicament.

'I'm looking for a specific man, one who won't disappoint me by not being able to answer simple questions.'

As the two men floundered in finding an answer to that, Jim moved down the bar.

'Are these men annoying you?' he asked.

One man turned to face him while the other man decided that conversation wasn't as much fun as holding her. He moved in to grab her arm again, but before he could even touch her, a resounding slap to the cheek knocked him sideways.

'They are, but I can take care of myself,' she said, batting her hands together. Then, when the man had shaken off the blow and moved in again, she jerked a knee up fast and hard.

Jim didn't see where it landed, but he couldn't help but wince when the man bleated in pain, then fell to his knees. The other man decided this was a good moment to leave.

'I can see that,' Jim said as laughter rang out around the saloon, that laughter growing when the stricken man keeled over on to his side. 'But if you promise not to give me the same treatment, I'll try to help you with your simple question.'

Although Jim put on a winning smile, she still considered him haughtily, as if this was an unlikely possibility.

'I'm looking for someone who I'd heard had come to Carmon,' she said while looking around the saloon. 'He's called Jim Dragon.'

Jim smiled. 'I might be able to find this Jim Dragon, but I hope he doesn't disappoint you.'

Her gaze rested on him. She narrowed her eyes.

'If you're him, he already has.'

Ten minutes later they were sitting in

the eatery beside the saloon and she was demolishing a plate of beefsteak and potatoes with a speed that confirmed she'd been on the trail for a while.

'So why have you ridden for so long just to find someone as disappointing as me?' he asked.

'Believe me, I wasn't looking for you specifically,' she said between mouthfuls, 'but when I heard you were here, I thought you might be the man I need.'

'Why?'

'I saw your wagon and heard about the bones you'd brought back from your latest exploit.' She uttered a peal of laughter. 'I see you're still using the old trick with the false bottom.'

Jim couldn't help but return a snort of laughter and now that he knew where this meeting might be heading, he began eating.

'We've met before?'

'I saw you from a distance, briefly, some years ago. I'm Emily and you met my father, Seymour Chambers.'

Jim continued eating while he sifted through memories of the many hundreds of men he'd dealt with until an image of Seymour came. He gulped down a potato, then looked aloft as he quoted the last words Seymour had said to him.

' 'You're a two-bit good-for-nothing leech, who is tarnishing the legacy of noble creatures you cannot comprehend. The sooner your type become extinct the better the world will be and I'll breathe easier knowing the air is no longer polluted by your foul stench'.'

'Don't worry.' She munched a mouthful of steak. 'He said that to all the bone hunters, but that never stopped him from using them when they had something he wanted.'

'And how is dear old Seymour?'

'Dead.' She waited while he murmured the most sincere sounding consolation he could muster. 'Or at least I think he is, but that's where you come in. He hasn't returned from his latest expedition.'

'I hunt long dead bones, not . . . not people.'

'In this case perhaps you can combine the two.'

Jim forked a slice of beef then released the fork to leave it pointing upwards while he pondered. He had been planning to rest up for a while, enjoying the benefits of his hard work.

On the other hand Pierre Dulaine would have uncovered his duplicity by now and be on his trail. Moving elsewhere quickly might be wise.

'Go on,' he said, still undecided.

'Pa heard about an old map an explorer had made that detailed the location of some massive lizard bones in Devil's Canyon north of Bear Creek. He went and . . . ' Her voice broke and she put down her utensils. She took deep breaths before continuing in a softer voice. 'He never goes for this long without getting word back to me.'

As travelling to Bear Creek would take him back into Pierre's territory, Jim blew out his cheeks, searching for the right words. When they wouldn't come he decided to just say it straight.

'That's a mighty intriguing story, but not intriguing enough.'

'The bones will be valuable.'

'I'm sure they will be, but I'm not short of money right now.'

She offered a tentative smile. 'The journey isn't that far and I reckon you could do with moving on.'

'I could, but not to Devil's Canyon. To the south, where Pierre Dulaine never goes, is where I need to be.' He frowned. 'I'm sorry.'

She considered him, then gave a dismissive shrug and poked her meal.

'Then I'll have to find someone else to take me there.'

Jim winced. 'You intend to go on this expedition yourself?'

'Of course.'

Jim cast a crafty glance down from her face then back up.

'Why didn't you say so earlier?' he said, holding out a hand.

3

'Stop,' Nathaniel said.

Cooper Metcalf responded to the order in the docile and stunned way that most men did after they'd just received the news they were likely to spend the rest of their life in jail.

The anger would come later. But by then Nathaniel and Shackleton aimed to be far away from Bear Creek and to be in control of the situation.

Sheriff Bryce and Deputy Albright followed the prisoner down the steps from the courthouse. Ahead were the cells and to the right was the door through which anyone who had been found innocent would go.

Despite the thirty years Judge Matthews had just handed down, when Bryce had completed the paperwork, Cooper would be going to the right. As the sheriff busied himself, the others stood guard around him.

'You planning to give us a hard time?' Shackleton said, standing up close to the prisoner.

'No,' Cooper murmured with a broken voice that confirmed his shock.

'That's good for you, because our orders are to deliver you to the gates of Beaver Ridge jail. They don't say what state you have to be in, just that you have to be alive enough to enjoy their hospitality. So you try anything, I'll beat you to pulp. Try anything again, I'll put a bullet in you. Understand?'

Anger flared in Cooper's eyes. 'I'd prefer death to jail.'

Shackleton laughed. 'You sure? I can make living worse.'

Cooper lowered his head as Deputy Albright grabbed his arm and moved him on to Bryce's desk. Nathaniel caught Shackleton's eye before they followed.

'I thought,' Nathaniel whispered, 'it was my turn to be the nasty one.'

'But you do the nice guy so well.'

Nathaniel smiled, then moved on. While Shackleton signed for Cooper, Nathaniel knelt. They would be riding so he removed the prisoner's leg irons, although he would keep the handcuffs on. Then he took hold of the chain connecting his cuffs and moved him round to face the door.

'We're going outside, then straight to our horses,' he said. 'We'll mount up and move out before anyone knows you've gone. Keep quiet and it'll work out fine.'

Nathaniel provided a reassuring smile that Cooper didn't return, although he gave a brief nod that confirmed they would maintain a cordial relationship while Shackleton delivered the threats.

When Shackleton slipped the papers into his pocket, Nathaniel tugged the prisoner on, but Albright stepped forward.

'I'm coming with you,' he said.

'We work alone,' Shackleton said, with Nathaniel muttering his support.

36

As Albright shrugged with a gesture that said he was as unhappy with this change of plan as they were, Bryce came out from behind his desk. Bryce considered Shackleton, his firm-set jaw acknowledging that as they worked for the governor of Beaver Ridge jail, he couldn't give them orders.

'If you insist, he stays here,' he said, 'but I reckon he'd benefit from working with two men who know the proper way to deal with a prisoner.'

'So,' Shackleton said as Albright lowered his head, 'this is the man you left on duty when Cooper took his short trip outside?'

'He is.' Bryce sighed. 'But that'll be his last mistake as my deputy, one way or the other. I'd prefer the way that stops me having to hire someone else.'

Shackleton considered the disgraced deputy, then nodded. With that concluding the debate, he then ignored the unwelcome new arrival as he and Nathaniel carried out a procedure they'd already perfected on the previous times they'd taken prisoners out of town unseen.

They slipped outside, went to their horses at the back of the courthouse where nobody was around, then headed away from town without even being noticed. The scuffling of feet and the raised voices of the people emerging from the court and then congregating outside the jailhouse sounded behind them, but they heard no suggestion that anyone had seen them leave.

They still took no chances and when they were out of view from the town they speeded up and took one of their many roundabout routes to Devil's Canyon.

Nathaniel drew back to watch Cooper in case he tried anything, while Shackleton rode alongside the prisoner. Although he'd not been given instructions, Albright rode in a casual manner, only rarely looking at the prisoner, suggesting the reason why Cooper had been able to best him.

Nathaniel reckoned that at some point on this journey Albright would receive a rude awakening that would either make him or break him. Even though Shackleton was overplaying his gruff nature, he didn't suffer idiots for long.

As it turned out, they saw nobody and faced no problems that day. The sun had disappeared behind the far mountains when they made camp.

They chose a high spot where they could look back towards the entrance to Devil's Canyon and the creek below, but here they could also see anyone approaching. The wind whipped flurries of dust around their ankles. The lack of cloud promised a cold night.

Albright took care of the horses while Shackleton laid out the rules for the night to Cooper. With his sentence having been delivered some hours ago and with that time having been spent outdoors, which he would probably never see again, he was more animated than before.

The two men had seen this type of behaviour many times and they knew what to expect, but that didn't mean they'd be complacent. When they'd settled down, Shackleton turned his attention on to the main unknown element on their trip.

'So, Deputy Albright,' he said, 'you're here to learn how to stop prisoners escaping, are you?'

Albright bit his lip, clearly stopping himself from snapping back the first retort that had come to mind. Despite his failure to do his duty that had almost led to Cooper being lynched, Nathaniel felt a twinge of sympathy for his predicament. He would have had to swallow his pride, and the fact that he had done so showed a laudable desire to become a better law officer.

'Bryce reckons I need to learn from the best,' Albright said.

'Do you?'

'I do.' He looked at Nathaniel then back to Shackleton. 'I'll decide later whether I have done.'

Nathaniel drew in his breath, ending his brief feeling of empathy for Albright's situation, but Shackleton smiled.

'That's the first thing you've said or done that gives me hope you'll succeed. Trust nobody but yourself and those who have proved themselves to you.'

'I intend to,' Albright said, his tone relaxing from its previous tenseness. He turned to the prisoner. 'And I trust that one least of all after he sneaked past me.'

Shackleton winked at Nathaniel, acknowledging that he was passing up the opportunity to berate him for his stupid mistake.

'Trust nothing anyone does or says goes double for prisoners.'

Albright continued to glare at Cooper. 'Except for the one thing we all want to hear.'

This comment made Cooper look at him, then deliver a slow shake of the head.

'Which is?' Shackleton asked.

'Cooper's never talked about what he did. That means Narcissa's body is still missing. We'd all like to know what he did with her.'

Anger flared in Cooper's eyes before he looked away. Shackleton said nothing, maintaining his gruff demeanour, letting Nathaniel make the obvious comment.

'We won't be questioning the prisoner about anything,' he said.

'There's a dead woman lying out there somewhere,' Albright snapped, pointing down into Devil's Canyon. 'Don't you care about that?'

'I do, but getting answers isn't our responsibility. We treat him well and deliver him to jail. That's our duty, nothing else.'

Albright muttered something to himself before shrugging.

'If you won't do anything but carry out your orders, then there's nothing I can say that'll give you a conscience.' His tone was terse, suggesting the matter wouldn't end here.

'Getting too involved leads to sloppiness,' Shackleton said. 'Put your personal feelings aside and concentrate on your duty.'

Albright opened his mouth, a finger rising to punctuate his point, but then he thought better of making it and conceded Shackleton's comment with a nod.

'I made a mistake back in the jailhouse.' Albright clenched his hands into tight fists. 'It won't happen again. But that won't stop me caring about the town I've sworn to protect.'

'Nobody said you had to.' Shackleton rubbed his hands. 'And if that matter is over, it leaves the question of how we use you.'

'Tell me the plan and I'll help as best I can,' Albright said, his tone softening now that he'd delivered an outburst that had clearly been building up for a while.

Shackleton nodded. 'We usually head along alternating sides of Devil's Canyon, but this time we're going the same way as last time. It's a slower route, but if anyone saw us take Washington Cody to jail they won't expect that.'

'I caught Washington, so I'm pleased you delivered him safely.' Albright considered. 'Clearly you're used to working as a twosome, so I could scout around and look for trouble.'

'You do that. Scout around.'

Albright thanked him, although Nathaniel reckoned he hadn't understood Shackleton's intent. The route along the westward side of the canyon was thin and treacherous, often leaving room for the travellers to go only forward or back. They could cover both directions between them and so giving him a roving brief merely ensured he didn't get in their way.

With their discussions concluded, they settled down for the night. The prisoner lay in the centre of the camp while they took up positions around him. Shackleton allocated Albright the first duty watch and the last.

This ensured that they'd both be awake for most of Albright's first watch, but Nathaniel didn't sleep. Throughout the day his duty had occupied his mind and he hadn't had time to ponder about his need to ensure this mission's success.

When he took over from Albright he had reached no firm decisions other than that he should lose himself in the work and not worry.

The deputy was in good spirits, this perhaps being the first thing he'd done right since yesterday's disastrous escape. That observation helped to firm Nathaniel's resolution to treat this mission as any other. He would concentrate on the task's minutiae and so ensure he kept up his guard and avoided slipups.

Within moments of ending his duty Albright was snoring, those snores gradually being joined by the prisoner's snores and then Shackleton's lighter breathing. As it turned out, the night shifts passed without incident and after

Nathaniel turned to Albright for the final time he quickly fell into a deep sleep.

A timeless period later Shackleton shook Nathaniel's shoulder and woke him. He sat up, instantly awake, and sought out Cooper. The prisoner was stirring, but he was doing so sleepily. Then he looked to Shackleton, who was scowling.

'What's wrong?' Nathaniel asked.

'It's Deputy Albright,' Shackleton snapped. 'He's gone.'

★　★　★

Bear Creek hadn't changed since the last time Jim Dragon had visited. This time, though, he had a companion, so he didn't head straight for the saloon.

Despite his concern about the possibility of Pierre Dulaine tracking him down and the beguiling possibilities of accompanying Emily, the journey had been quiet. He had seen no sign of his rival and after being animated in

46

Carmon, Emily had been subdued, presumably as she contemplated the likely unwelcome conclusion to her quest.

They pulled up outside Martha's Eatery, but the establishment was closed. It was around noon so it should be open, but Jim's banging on the door failed to rouse anyone.

He returned to his wagon to report the bad news, but Emily was leaning forward on her pinto, looking towards the edge of town. When he was up in the seat, he followed her gaze.

A commotion was in progress outside the jailhouse. People were emerging from around the side of the building while gesturing to each other and engaging in animated conversation.

'It looks as if most of the town is over there,' Emily said. 'We should find out what the trouble is.'

Jim noted the growing susurration of short comments, the raised arms, the angry faces. He'd seen mobs like this before.

'This is the kind of trouble we need to stay well clear of.'

'You stay here, then,' she muttered. She moved her horse on down the road. 'I want answers and I won't get them sitting around.'

Jim watched her leave until he was sure she was determined to mingle in with the crowd. Then, with a sigh, he trundled the wagon after her.

As the main bulk of people were now walking purposefully towards them, she soon reached the gathering. They both parted the crowd, but with the people pressing in on all sides she dismounted and started asking questions.

The first person she asked provided an answer that made her put a hand to her mouth. Then she mounted back up and with a kick and a shake of the reins she urged the horse on. Cries of alarm went up, but she still rode on through the people forcing them to dive and scurry out of the way.

Jim followed at a more sedate pace as the fallen got to their feet and glared at her receding back. But they soon rejoined the procession in heading down the road.

Emily carried on until she reached the stables, the last building on the road, where she jumped down from her horse and stomped to the end of the boardwalk. She sat on the edge then stood and sat again, her actions jerky and angry.

Jim slowed down to give her time to calm down, but when he reached her she was red-faced and her fists were clenched tightly as she looked for something to take out her anger on. Jim decided to risk being that something and he jumped down from the wagon to join her.

'The questioning not go well, then?' he asked, using a breezy tone to help speed up the inevitable outburst, but instead she just set her chin on her hands and looked up at him with a resigned air.

'All this effort to find you, then to come here, and it's been wasted.'

Jim glanced at the crowd. It was now gathering outside a saloon where someone had appointed himself as spokesman and was standing on the boardwalk making a speech. Jim couldn't hear the words, but it made the crowd cheer.

'What did that man say?'

'That things are about to turn real ugly. They're planning to lynch Cooper Metcalf. Apparently he's already on his way to Beaver Ridge jail, but they know which way he's been taken.'

'And why should that concern you?'

'Because Cooper Metcalf was the man my father came here to see.'

'I'm sorry,' Jim said with a sympathetic tone. He joined her on the edge of the boardwalk. 'It seems your father met up with an evil man.'

She opened her mouth then closed it and glanced away, suggesting that that hadn't been her concern. She took a minute before she replied, during which time several more cheers sounded from the crowd as they goaded each other on to chase after Cooper.

'I'd already accepted he was dead, but Cooper is the one man who might know something, and now I won't be able to question him.'

Jim offered a hopeful smile. 'I'm a bone hunter. I find things nobody else can. This doesn't end here.'

She picked up a handful of pebbles and absently threw them to the ground one at a time.

'It does. I'm sorry. I shouldn't have got you involved.'

'But you have, and you have nothing to apologize about. Whether you give up or not, I'll still search up in Devil's Canyon.'

She shrugged then returned to throwing pebbles.

'Don't worry about me,' she murmured, her voice choking up. 'You go and look for your bones.'

Lost for the right thing to say he said nothing, but the set of her shoulders suggested that even when she recovered from her shock, she wouldn't stay with him.

He glanced over his shoulder at the crowd that was now purposefully moving away. Then, as she was trying and failing to fight back the sniffles, he looked out of town.

Several riders were approaching. They were a quarter-mile away, but something about their postures tapped at his mind. He narrowed his eyes, an uncomfortable thought growing. Then he winced.

'Pierre Dulaine,' he murmured.

She swung round to him, wiping her cheeks, her tense jaw showing that she was forcing herself to concentrate on something other than her own problems.

'The man you double-crossed back in Carmon?'

'I don't see it that way, but he sure will. I need to get moving.' He stood. 'It's decision time, Emily. Come with me now or stay.'

She glanced at the approaching riders

then at the dispersing crowd. She gave a short nod, then slapped her legs and stood.

'I've come too far to give up without a fight.'

'Good,' Jim said, turning to his wagon. 'We need to hide before Pierre sees me.'

'Where?' she asked, joining him.

Jim stopped beside his wagon and considered the mob. He smiled.

'In the one place he won't expect me to be.'

4

'Deputy Albright couldn't find his way around his own jailhouse,' Shackleton said. 'So how could he sneak away without us hearing him?'

Nathaniel scowled and again ran his gaze over the surrounding area, but the deputy was long gone. Their prisoner was secure, but that hadn't helped to lighten either man's mood.

'And why did he go?' Nathaniel said.

'He sounded more concerned about finding out where Narcissa's body was than guarding our prisoner, so perhaps he lost interest when we refused to help him.'

'Perhaps, but leaving us won't help him get any answers.'

'Or then again it might be the only way he will get answers.' Shackleton stood over their prisoner. 'You ready to ride hard to avoid whatever Albright's planned?'

A momentary shocked look came over Cooper's eyes before he blinked it away, showing that recent events hadn't knocked all the fight out of him.

'If he's determined to make me talk about Narcissa,' he said, 'even if he has to abandon his duty and kidnap me, then that fate will be a better one than a drawn-out living death in Beaver Ridge.'

For long moments Shackleton considered him. Then, with a grunt of irritation, he gestured to Nathaniel to take care of him.

Within minutes they moved off from the camp. Only when they were riding along the rim of Devil's Canyon did Shackleton broach the subject that was on Nathaniel's mind too.

'Albright could have mislaid the key to Cooper's cell to let him escape so he could bypass the law. So if he's not as stupid as he appeared, he'll be up to no good again. And he knows the route we're taking.'

'If we stick to the same route, anyone he talks to could find us easily. But he might expect us to go up the other side of the canyon, so it might be best to stick to the original route ... ' Nathaniel snorted a harsh laugh. 'We could tie ourselves up in knots over this, so we should only worry about what we know.'

'Which is nothing. Albright left us, but we don't know why for sure, so we don't second-guess ourselves.'

The two men exchanged brief nods, and with that being the extent of the debate they needed they rode on along the top of the canyon.

When they next stopped they were twenty miles beyond the mouth of the canyon, high on the western side. Down below was the blue ribbon of the winding creek that ultimately swung round to flow by Bear Creek.

The opposite side of the canyon was a quarter-mile away. With there being only a few, and then not well-known, routes down to the base of the canyon, anyone who was on that side and who wanted to waylay them would already face a long journey to reach them. And that situation would become more beneficial the further they travelled.

As the route ahead swung off around an extended outcrop, this would be the last time they would have a clear view back towards Bear Creek. So the two men moved as close to the edge as was safe. Then, with their hands to their brows, they surveyed the horizon.

Shackleton grunted a moment before Nathaniel saw the large but distant dust cloud.

'Trouble,' Nathaniel said.

'Several hours away,' Shackleton said.

'True, but they're on this side of the canyon.'

Shackleton gave a grim nod. Then they gestured for their prisoner to move on as they sought to put distance between themselves and whoever was following them.

'The usual places?' Shackleton asked when they reached the outcrop.

Nathaniel considered. It appeared that Deputy Albright had told others about their route, but he knew nothing about their procedures other than the sketchy details they'd relayed last night.

'The usual places,' he said.

★ ★ ★

'Do you reckon they'll give up too?' Emily said.

'It doesn't look like it,' Jim said. 'Cooper Metcalf's riled them up.'

Emily firmed her jaw, then returned to glaring at the riders around them. There were around thirty in the group, although another twenty had started with them.

By mid-afternoon these people had fallen back, then swung round to return to town, most without providing excuses, leaving only the men who looked as if they'd never relent.

With Emily still being upset, she had agreed to ride with him on the wagon. Her horse was tethered behind.

Of Pierre Dulaine they'd seen no sign.

They'd managed to leave town before he arrived and nobody had followed the group. Still, Jim had resolved to stay with them for as long as they were going in the same direction as he'd intended to go.

Cooper Metcalf might not be able to help them now, but a quest with which he was more familiar would begin soon, although before he left the group he hoped he'd be able to probe for details about Cooper's exploits. He got the chance when in mid-afternoon they reached the base of the canyon.

The group leader deemed this a good moment to rest, so, as they watered their horses in the creek, Jim milled in with the others and in his usual casual way he probed for answers.

'You reckon we'll catch him tonight?' he asked a dour-faced man while he placed a wet kerchief on the back of his neck.

'Albright reckons it'll take another full day.'

The man's brief head-nudge indicated the group's leader. This was the nearest Jim had come to him and he noticed that he wore a deputy's badge. He had been under the impression that this pursuit wasn't an official one.

'I doubt there's any trees up at the canyon.'

The man snorted a laugh.

'We're not in that much of a hurry. We'll bring him back and let him sweat so he'll answer Albright's questions.' He considered him. His eyes narrowed as the obvious thought hit him. 'I don't know you. Why are you after Cooper?'

'It's a long story.' Jim removed the kerchief, then wrung it out and wet it again in a show of not having enough time to explain.

Seeing that he wasn't going to continue, the man glanced further along the side of the creek to Emily. He cocked his head to one side.

'But I know her. Can't think where. I've seen her though.' He rubbed his jaw. 'Years ago, I reckon.'

His gaze made Emily look their way and she beamed an innocent smile before returning to the wagon. The man moved to follow her, so Jim relented with a little information.

'She's the reason we joined,' he said, halting him. 'Cooper might know what happened to her father. Perhaps before you string him up he might talk about that too.'

The man furrowed his brow. 'There should be enough time, but you'll have to check with Albright.'

Before Jim could probe further Deputy Albright hollered for everyone to restart the pursuit. So, in short order, everyone hurried back to their mounts. Emily was already in position when he reached the wagon.

He flashed her an encouraging smile, then shook the reins and moved the wagon into line. Slowly the train of riders moved out. When they were trundling along, she slapped her legs with a gesture that he now knew meant she'd been thinking and had made a decision.

'I'd like to stay with these people for a while,' she said. 'Cooper might know something useful.'

Jim winced. 'He might do, but these people aim to lynch him. That won't be a pretty sight.'

He drew her attention to two men who were dallying beside the water. They were avoiding catching anyone's eyes with a look that said they were ashamed and that they didn't want to explain that they were turning back.

She shrugged and resorted to silence. That being the extent of the debate, Jim presumed that later he'd relent and they'd end up riding with this group. He noticed that both men who had left were riding buggies leaving him as the only one with a wagon, a fact that might give him an advantage he could use later.

A mile on, the man he'd spoken to moved alongside another man. They spoke. Then they both looked back at the wagon.

Jim presumed they were discussing him and his reason for joining the group, but Emily squirmed on her seat and looked elsewhere. He waited until both men had turned away.

'They seemed interested in you,' he said.

She pointed along the trail. 'I'm the only woman left.'

'Then don't worry. You'll be safe with me.'

'I know. Despite what they're planning to do, these are good people.' She glanced at him, then chuckled. 'I have been to Bear Creek before.'

Jim smiled, relieved she'd broached this subject first.

'When?'

'I came with Father four years ago. I used to accompany him on his travels until I decided that examining what he found was more interesting than the finding.'

Jim gestured at the two men. 'You

must have made a big impression if they remember a young girl who just passed through four years ago.'

She lowered her head, her face reddening.

'I did,' she said with a cough. 'But I'm more responsible now.'

'A pity,' he said. She didn't look at him and he decided to store that information away to use later.

The group carried on past a sprawling spread of houses, identified as Wilson's Crossing. Emily looked at the houses as they passed, her gaze preoccupied, presumably with the thought that this might be the last sign of civilization they would see for a while.

They rode up the side of the canyon, steadily gaining height, then along the rim. The ground was hard and nobody was able to find tracks to confirm they were on the right track. But when they'd settled down for the night the group turned out to be a lively bunch, who put aside their grim duty to gather around the fire and chat.

Emily stayed close to Jim and didn't mix, her return to quietness making Jim pensive. They slept on the back of the wagon and in the morning Jim faced the decision on whether they should stay with the group or make their own way.

Emily was still hopeful that she might be able to question Cooper, if they ever caught up with him. Judging that he could start exploring the canyon at any time, Jim agreed.

They rode on through the morning with the deepening canyon to one side and at times a sheer rock face to the other that left them with a treacherous path to traverse in single file. Although Jim had been assured there was enough room for the wagon, often the wheels rolled along only feet from the edge.

As there was often a sheer drop of hundreds of feet to one side of the path, Emily sat on the further side from the rim, and Jim found himself sliding along closer to her. They didn't catch sight of their quarries, but whenever they stopped Albright's confidence that they would catch up with Cooper kept everyone in a good mood.

Sundown was approaching on the second day of the journey when Albright drew everyone to a halt. They were in a rare wider section of the path along the canyon top. Jim presumed they were to settle down here for the night, but Albright had other ideas.

'Are we ready to get him now?' he asked.

'Yes!' several people said, shaking fists and brandishing guns, although once they'd displayed their bravado their gazes strayed to the route ahead. Along the long sweep of the canyon there was no sign of anyone.

'Then we stay quiet for now, split up, and before the moon rises, we'll have Cooper Metcalf.'

5

'I suppose this'll be another cold night,' Cooper grumbled.

'You'd better get used to them,' Nathaniel said. 'In Beaver Ridge the wind whistles through the cells worse than this.'

Cooper scowled, then reverted to silence, leaving Nathaniel and Shackleton to organize themselves. They had chosen a spot in which they'd camped before, keeping to their original plan of not letting Albright's disappearance cause them to panic.

It was a gully with only one entrance and it was situated away from the canyon edge. The narrow entrance ensured that it was only noticeable to anyone passing by if they knew it was there, and the steep sides meant the entrance was the only way to approach them. It was a place they could defend easily, although that had never proved necessary before.

Shackleton took up a position by the entrance, where he could see anyone passing by, while Nathaniel sat with the prisoner. Night had fallen before either man spoke again.

'When do we get there?' Cooper asked.

'Early afternoon, the day after tomorrow,' Nathaniel said.

'And then you move on while your victims can't move anywhere?'

Nathaniel shuffled round to sit facing Cooper. Now that the sun had set he had only enough light to see his outline, but he still offered a smile. After two days' treating the prisoner reasonably, while Shackleton delivered bluster and sharp orders, it wasn't surprising that he would now want to talk.

Tomorrow Cooper would be even friendlier if he followed the usual process the prisoners went through, as he tried to win Nathaniel's confidence and hope to lull him into making a mistake.

'We don't make decisions on who is guilty,' Nathaniel said. 'We just do our job and we treat our charges as best we can.'

'Then you're no better than the lawmen who arrest innocent men.'

Nathaniel nodded. 'We're not, but we don't claim to be. We do, though, understand the problem.'

'I understand it too,' Cooper snapped with a rattle of his hand chain. 'Except if I were in your position, I'd do the right thing.'

Over by the entrance Shackleton looked at them, so, clearly, they were speaking too loudly.

'I have been in your position,' Nathaniel said, lowering his voice. 'And I knew then that the people who guarded me were just doing their duty.'

Cooper raised his eyebrows in surprise at this revelation.

'Perhaps they did in your case, but it's different for me. I didn't kill

Narcissa and neither did Washington kill her father. That should have been obvious to anyone who knew us, but somehow you've ended up escorting two innocent men to jail.'

'And we'll make sure you get there, as we did with Washington.'

Cooper glared at Nathaniel, then, with a muttered oath to himself, he slapped his hands on his knees and shuffled round to face the entrance.

'I'm not wasting my breath talking to you. You'll never understand.'

Nathaniel stood and moved over to look down at him before he took up his position by the side of the gully.

'Perhaps I won't, but that doesn't mean I won't listen. We'll treat you properly and also defend you from anyone who wants to deliver a more immediate form of justice.' Nathaniel gestured around. 'So you can rest assured that you'll be as safe as you can be.'

'Nobody knows about this gully, then?' Cooper said with a hurt voice

70

that said that whatever he had hoped to achieve by talking to him had failed, but that he still wanted to continue talking.

'Yes. It's a secret place.'

Cooper snorted. 'Then how come I know about it?'

Nathaniel shrugged. 'It's fairly secret, then. Albright doesn't know we stop here.'

Cooper nodded and was silent for a while, appearing as if he wouldn't speak again. Accordingly Nathaniel sat on a boulder.

'Who does know you stop here?' Cooper asked in a low tone.

'Very few. We don't talk about our procedures with others.'

'But who?' Cooper leaned forward.

'I guess the governor of Beaver Ridge jail — '

'Idiots!' Cooper snapped. 'Governor Bradbury is the one person you should never tell anything.'

He said no more, but even given his understandable opinion about people in authority, his reaction had seemed to be

71

more than just hatred. Nathaniel turned to Shackleton, aiming to suggest they find somewhere else to camp this night, but Shackleton had slipped out through the entrance, something he would do only if there was trouble.

'Stay,' Nathaniel muttered, although there was nowhere that Cooper could go.

He edged along the side of the gully to the entrance and peered out. The rock wall was ahead before it swung away towards the canyon. There was no sign of Shackleton. He listened, but he heard nothing.

This wasn't unusual as Shackleton could slip through the darkness like the wind, but several minutes passed in which the only noise was the intermittent rustling of dust. He looked back at Cooper. He was sitting hunched and withdrawn in a position where he could see him if he went out, so he moved on.

With his back to the rock, he sidestepped to the corner. He again checked on Cooper, then edged slowly around the corner. The view beyond opened up to let him see the land beyond the canyon rim, but there was no sign of Shackleton.

Shaking his head, he turned back, trusting that his partner knew what he was doing. When he rounded the corner, Cooper was still showing no interest in proceedings, so he moved to rejoin him.

Something flittered at the edge of his vision, the movement of a dark object over the shadows.

Nathaniel flinched away from it, saving himself from a looped rope that slapped to the ground beside his right foot. He looked up to see the outlines of two men peering down into the gully, fifty feet up. One man made a gesture to someone out of his view, showing that others had arrived and perhaps that they had already subdued Shackleton.

He hurried back into the gully just as Cooper looked up. A rope spiralled down to the ground to his side from above. He jerked away from it, but that only moved him into the path of a third rope from the other side of the gully.

It slipped down around his neck in a terrible foreshadowing of the fate the attackers had planned for him before it carried on down to his shoulders. Cooper twisted and struggled, but with his hands chained together he couldn't shake it off, and instead the rope drew up tight around his chest.

While looking up into the darkness, Nathaniel hurried to him. He counted five men on the edge of the gully, looking down. The gully was deeper at the back and the rope was at the full extent of its reach, giving Nathaniel hope that he might be able to fight them off.

He joined Cooper as a second man joined the first rope-holder in his attempt to reel the prisoner in, but when Nathaniel grabbed Cooper they both took up the strain, which stopped Cooper from being moved. Then they dragged the two rope-holders closer to the edge where, seeing that they were in danger of being pulled down, they both released the rope.

With the tension gone from the rope, Cooper and Nathaniel stumbled backwards. Nathaniel managed to stop himself falling, but Cooper went to his knees. Nathaniel helped him up, then directed him to hide in the shadows at the side of the gully. He'd managed only a few paces when, with a rustle, another rope came looping down.

This rope slid down over Nathaniel's wrist. He had to holster his gun to peel it away before it could tighten, but as it turned out that had been only a distraction.

Two more ropes came swinging down. One missed Cooper by several feet, but the second landed around his shoulders and drew tight.

Again Nathaniel joined Cooper and they both put hand to rope and tried to keep the ropers at bay, but this time four men had taken the strain at the other end. Inexorably they drew

Cooper towards the rocks, aiming to drag him up.

Nathaniel's feet left the ground, so he changed tactics and wrapped his arms around Cooper's chest, seeking to keep him down, but Cooper slipped from his grasp as he was raised. Nathaniel clutched his waist but that too moved higher, so he had no choice but to back away.

He drew his gun and centred it on the nearest man above.

'No further,' he demanded. 'Cooper's my prisoner.'

'You don't give the orders no longer, Nathaniel,' a voice said behind him.

He swirled round to see that Deputy Albright was walking into the gully with Shackleton walking ahead of him, trussed up in the way they'd tried to capture Cooper and himself.

'You're a sworn-in lawman,' Nathaniel said. 'So uphold the law and defy this lynch mob.'

Albright shrugged in an easy manner that removed the last doubts Nathaniel had that he was fully involved in this attack.

'I take care of the law, not you, and Cooper Metcalf is about to get the justice he deserves.'

Supportive grunts sounded from the men around the top of the gully and from the other men who filed in behind Shackleton.

'He'll get that, as decided by Judge Matthews. He'll spend as good as the rest of his life in Beaver Ridge jail.'

'And when he's there he won't talk about his crime and so a good woman's body will lie where he killed her.' Albright looked up at Cooper, who was now gently swinging a few feet off the ground. 'Except when that rope is no longer around his shoulders, he'll talk.'

'Getting that information isn't your responsibility.'

'It's not, but I've made it my duty.' Albright moved forward so that Nathaniel could see the crowd of men behind him, all of whom had drawn guns. 'And these men agree.'

Nathaniel looked around the gully. Men were above him, ropes at the ready, and Cooper had given up struggling. The only hope he could see was that these men were ordinary townsfolk who had been fired up by lurid tales of Cooper's crime. No matter what Albright said, they wouldn't want to kill someone who was only doing his duty.

'That doesn't matter. Back away and we'll say no more about this.'

Shackleton gave a brief nod, acknowledging he agreed with Nathaniel's stance, but Albright snorted.

'Stop pretending to be so noble. I know why you're really determined to risk everything to save him.' Albright smirked. 'If Cooper doesn't reach Beaver Ridge jail, then your fate is uncertain unless people speak up for you.'

Nathaniel firmed his jaw, unwilling to admit that this did worry him, even though his duty was his main concern.

'What you saying, Albright?'

'I'm giving you a plain offer. Force us

to take Cooper off you and your freedom will end. Say nothing about what happened here tonight and I'll support you.' Albright took a long pace forward. 'So, what's it to be, Nathaniel McBain?'

6

Deputy Albright had Cooper Metcalf.

He came down the side of the canyon with a hand clamped on his shoulder and with the others who had gone on the mission parading on either side. A cheer went up from the people who had stayed with Jim and Emily. Then they moved in to surround their prisoner.

Jim struggled to watch what happened next as everyone enjoyed goading their captive. They punched and shoved him. Then, when he fought his way clear and in anger delivered a swiping blow at one man with his chains, that prompted a sustained beating that knocked him to the ground, followed by kicks and scuffling.

Albright stood back, watching the proceedings with a smirk on his face. Only when the mob had knocked the fight out of Cooper did he step in. Even then he had to drag and push people aside.

'Enough!' he shouted. 'I want him alive enough to answer my questions.'

'Ask them now,' someone shouted. 'Then we can drag him back down the canyon behind a horse and hang whatever's left.'

This suggestion received a cheer. For a few terrible moments Albright grinned and Jim thought that was what they'd do, but then Albright shook his head.

'We stick to the plan. We keep him alive, for now.'

Grumbling disagreement greeted his declaration, but when Albright cast his measured gaze around the gathered people sounds of support started, then grew in volume. Albright dragged Cooper to his feet and the discussion about how they'd transport him back started.

Jim reckoned this was a good moment to step in, but he didn't need to when Albright directed the prisoner to his wagon.

'Bring him up here,' Jim still said, gesturing. 'We'll keep him safe.'

'We'll guard him,' Albright said.

He dragged the prisoner on past Jim and to the wagon.

'But I know my horses. He'll be safer with me.'

Albright stopped and let another man drag Cooper on to the back.

'We're obliged you've come, but nobody knows why you joined us. So we'll deal with him.'

Jim frowned then jerked his head to the side and walked away for a few paces. Albright followed.

'We're here because we have questions to ask Cooper too. Emily's father's gone missing.' Jim pointed at her, and she obligingly provided a meek and worried smile. 'Cooper might know something about that.'

Albright winced; when he spoke again his voice was low and distracted.

'I doubt Cooper would know anything about that. He was too busy killing Narcissa and trying to get away to attack anyone else.'

Jim snorted. 'You mean the notorious Cooper Metcalf, the most dangerous man in the state from the look of this mob, wouldn't have killed more than one person?'

His sarcasm made Albright narrow his eyes, but then he shrugged.

'If you want to waste your time asking questions he won't answer, you can. It might warm him up for answering mine.' He considered the wagon. 'Join us.'

'Obliged.' Jim moved over to take Emily's arm and escort her to the wagon before Albright could change his mind.

From the corner of his eye he saw Albright raise a hand and start to say that he meant only he could go, but Jim ignored him and helped her up.

When they were sitting on the wagon on the opposite side to the prisoner Albright joined them. Jim avoided catching the deputy's eye and checked that Emily was fine. But she ignored him and instead she stared at Cooper, who was lying where he'd fallen, her eyes wide with horror but also with compassion, presumably after witnessing his rough treatment.

Her concern for the man who might have been responsible for her father's disappearance touched Jim and he placed an arm around her shoulders. She murmured her thanks while Albright ordered another man to get on the seat and drive them back down the canyon.

With Albright sitting on one side of him and a burly guard on the other, Cooper grumbled to himself as he lay on his side, his legs drawn up in a defensive position in case the beatings continued.

The group prepared to move out. Not everyone who was still with the lynch mob was here. Despite his confidence after wresting Cooper from his guards, Albright had separated his forces in case the prisoner escaped. Some men had moved further along the canyon rim while others had stayed back, leaving ten people in the current group.

These people lined up before and behind the wagon. Then at a slow pace that gradually quickened they began the journey back down the canyon.

'When will you question him?' Emily asked Albright as they were trundling along.

'Later,' Albright said, 'but you can ask now.'

She nodded, then shuffled across the base of the wagon to sit beside Cooper. She laid a hand on his shoulder.

He flinched away as if it were a blow, but she placed it down again and this time he must have noticed the gentleness of her touch as he stayed put. Then slowly he looked up while keeping his head cringed against his shoulders, turtle-like.

He took in the positions of Albright and the other guard, both of whom hunched forward to glare at him. Then he considered Jim sitting on the other side of the wagon. Jim gave him a supportive nod.

Cooper nodded back, suggesting he had been paying enough attention to know he had spoken reasonably and so wouldn't harm him. He took a deep breath, then looked at Emily.

'You met my father,' Emily said, speaking quickly. 'He left to explore Devil's Canyon a month ago, but he hasn't returned. Do you know anything about that?'

'I have no idea what you mean,' Cooper murmured, looking her over with wide eyes, presumably in surprise at finding a woman amongst the mob.

Emily let out a long breath, relieving the tension she must be feeling, and looked away into the darkness of the canyon, her eyes sad.

Albright grunted with irritation.

'Talk to the lady,' he snarled, kicking Cooper's leg. 'Or I'll make this journey the longest of your life.'

Cooper lowered his head. He ignored a second kick and a slap to the back of the head from the second guard.

'Don't,' Emily said. 'I'm sure he has

some good in him, and treating him badly won't make him talk.'

Albright laughed. 'Wait until we stop for the night. Then you'll see how I can make a man talk.'

She leaned forward. 'Please, Cooper, everyone's angry, so make this easy on yourself and help me. You wrote to him about having found a map in the canyon. He came to see you. I've not seen him again, but he might not have even reached you. Please.'

Cooper looked up to consider her pleading expression. His stern-jawed expression softened as he fingered a scrape on his cheek and then his bloodied lip.

'Your father is Seymour Chambers?'

'Yes. Did you meet him?'

Cooper bit his lip. He looked at Albright, who leaned towards him, the set of his shoulders backing up his earlier threats.

'Help me to sit up and I'll tell you,' he said.

Cooper held out a hand to Emily, but

Albright moved round to grab his arm. With much groaning on Cooper's part, he dragged him up to sit with his back to the sideboard. Cooper raised his hat to run his manacled hands through his hair and glanced around.

They were moving steadily down the side of the canyon. It was a treacherous section before they reached a wider area where, presumably, Albright would let them make camp.

Behind them riders were just visible in the low light and ahead the riders had disappeared from view around a rock. The driver was keeping the horses on a tight rein as he negotiated a corner that Jim could remember as presenting a worrying sight even in full light.

'And?' Emily prompted leaning forward until she was on her knees facing him.

Cooper leaned forward. He whispered something in her ear that made her sit upright. Then he raised his manacles and gave them an aggrieved look.

The wagon shook as the driver manoeuvred around the treacherous corner, making everyone lurch.

Cooper took advantage of the motion and leaped to the side, swinging the manacles up.

His sudden movement took Albright by surprise. The chain slapped him around the side of the head, cracking his head back. He raised a hand to his face, but that only gave Cooper the room to slap him again. This time Albright toppled backwards over the side of the wagon.

The second guard lunged forward and grabbed Cooper's wrists. He pushed them down while he wrapped his other arm around his neck and dragged him down to the base of the wagon. Cooper bunched his shoulders, then tried to throw the man off, but instead his assailant rested his weight on him, keeping him subdued.

Shouting went up from behind as the following riders slowed to help Albright. While the guard kept the situation under control Jim moved round the two of them to ensure Emily was safe. But when he reached her, she pushed him away.

'This is wrong,' she said. 'Help him.'

Jim glanced at the tussling men. Cooper's rediscovered strength had faded away and the guard was keeping him pinned down with ease.

'It is,' Jim said, 'but we can't do anything.'

She sneered. 'You might not, but I will.'

With a determined move she swung away to the front of the wagon. The driver's concentration was on negotiating the tight corner, so he didn't react as she got to her feet and walked up to him.

She stood behind him, then slapped both hands down on his shoulders and dragged him backwards. The blow was clearly a shock as his back rebounded from the seat and he went reeling to the side. Emily took advantage of his surprise and shoved him forward.

The man kept a firm grip of the reins, but this proved to be his downfall as the horses surged on around the corner and dragged him forward. Unbalanced he toppled from view as with a calm movement Emily stepped over into the seat and reached for the reins.

She gathered them up, then cast Jim a look before sitting down. The guard had heard the altercation and he looked up, giving Cooper enough leeway to mount a fight back, although he was still on his knees on the base of the wagon.

Behind, the riders had stretched out as they carefully rounded the corner. Jim considered them, then Emily, then Cooper. He shrugged, judging that there was no pleasant outcome to this situation.

He stepped over to the guard and grabbed his upper arm. Then he moved to drag him off Cooper, but the man shook him away. Jim tried again, gathering a firmer grip, and threw the man across the wagon.

A gunshot rattled, spraying splinters from the sideboard a foot away from his right hand.

The riders had now negotiated the corner and they had the wagon in their sights. Jim moved for his gun as a more sustained volley ripped out. Again it tore into the sideboard, and this time he accepted they weren't actually aiming at him, that it was a warning, for now.

As Cooper had thrown himself across the wagon at the guard, their pursuers wouldn't want to risk hitting their man, and they probably didn't want Cooper to come to harm either before they hanged him.

Jim raised his hand from his holster, then turned on his heel, aiming to head to the front and persuade Emily to give up. But he saw that she didn't have a choice.

The riders they'd left further down the canyon were approaching and were blocking the trail between the sheer drop to the bottom of the canyon and the rocky side. Emily was urging the horses on, aiming to run them down, but the riders behind them were shouting out about what had happened, and they weren't moving aside.

'You can't run these people down,' Jim said when he reached the front. He leaned over the seat to catch her eye.

She glanced back at Cooper, who was now straining to push the guard over the side.

'I have to,' she said. 'Cooper said if I save him, he'll tell me about my father.'

'We'll find another way, one that'll get you answers and that won't end up with us joining Cooper on the end of a rope.'

She frowned, then gripped the reins more tightly and turned away.

'I have to do what's right,' she said.

Jim applauded her courage, but the riders ahead were blocking the trail with guns levelled on them and a determination in their postures that said they wouldn't let them pass. Then he saw a bigger problem.

Beyond the riders, four men had dismounted and they were toppling a boulder that had been lying to the side. It rolled on to land in the middle of the trail, its bulk promising to rip through the wagon if Emily tried to ride over it.

'You do, but not today,' Jim said. 'We're trapped both ways.'

Emily looked over her shoulder at the following riders, all packing guns and ready to overwhelm them the moment she stopped. Ahead the trail around the canyon rim veered to the side. Once it straightened, the boulder blocked the way.

'Then I'll go the other way!' she shouted, and with that she set the horses on a direct path towards the edge of the canyon.

The wagon trundled closer to the edge letting Jim see down into the canyon. There was nothing but darkness below.

7

'They couldn't have survived the fall,' Shackleton said, peering down into the canyon.

'Dead or not,' Nathaniel said, kneeling beside him, 'we have to deliver Cooper Metcalf to Beaver Ridge jail.'

'I was afraid you'd say that.' Shackleton stood back from the edge to consider the short length of canyon rim visible to them now that the moon had set. 'It'll take a while to get down there and find his body.'

Nathaniel nodded, pondering, as Shackleton was, on what their next actions should be.

Deputy Albright had taken their horses, leaving them afoot at the midway point between Bear Creek and Beaver Ridge. They had still followed on behind the lynch mob, and from some distance away they had heard their consternation.

So they had sneaked closer, planning to take on Albright, but when they had got close enough to overhear what had happened, they had decided to bide their time until he had moved on.

Now they faced a journey that in either direction would take several days before they reached a town, even without the added burden of finding then transporting Cooper's body.

Albright, though, had made one mistake: he had thought his threats were enough to buy their silence.

He was wrong.

They couldn't let him get away with his dereliction of duty. With that in mind Nathaniel turned towards Beaver Ridge.

'There's a way down a few miles on,' he said.

Shackleton set his hands on his hips as he considered. He gave a firm nod.

'There is,' he said as they set off, 'and when this is over, we'll teach Albright a lesson he'll never forget.'

The wagon was suspended in midair.

Jim had been watching it for a while, the sight being too bizarre for him to look away. Occasionally one of the wheels rolled back and forth, but it did so with a distinct wobble that made it appear ready to drop off.

Patiently Jim waited for the next wobble. He felt serene and watching the wheel was less troubling than his last fragmented memories.

Emily had hurtled along the top of the canyon far too quickly. An obstacle she couldn't avoid blocked their way, so she kept going in a straight line, heading on to the edge.

The horses protested, already spooked by the fast journey. Jim reckoned they'd turn, but the wagon was going so fast that he wasn't sure they could.

He clambered on to the seat, but he was already too late. A wheel slipped over the edge. For a frozen moment they carried on with three wheels on the ground. Then slowly they tipped to the side.

After that his memory would return to only brief moments.

He grabbed Emily. A jolt tore him loose and sent him into the back of the wagon. The guard tumbled over the side while Cooper reeled to the other side. He gained his feet. Ahead there was nothing but blackness and yet somehow the wagon was rolling down the side of an almost sheer drop.

He'd grabbed his lucky shark's tooth, and that was all he could remember. Yet now he was looking at the wagon, suspended there.

The wheel rocked again and this time it broke free and drifted serenely towards him. It grew larger as it approached and then the serenity ended when it spun away from his sight and a crash sounded.

He flinched, his perspective changing to let him see that he was lying on his back on the ground and the wagon was trapped between rocks a hundred feet above him.

He ventured to move and found that his limbs worked. Still feeling disorientated, he clambered to his feet. In a strange way he was grateful that his muscles creaked and a back spasm forced him to remain doubled over before he straightened.

The discomfort let him know that the situation was real and that somehow he had survived a plunge of several hundred feet to the canyon base.

He walked around in a circle, stretching his muscles and freeing the cramps. Several new bruises announced themselves, but they felt less constraining the more he moved. He walked to the broken wheel that had fallen then looked around.

The creek was fifty feet away, thundering by and foam-flecked. On this side of the creek the ground was flat, but it sloped away steeply on the other side. He looked up.

He was beneath the wagon, so he backtracked. By the time he was in a position where he would be safe if it were to fall he could see what had happened.

The canyon top was several hundred feet above, but, almost certainly by luck, the wagon had come over the side at a point where the ground sloped away less steeply than elsewhere. It was still almost a forty-five degree slope, but it had been shallow enough to let the wagon roll down for around a hundred feet. Deep gouges in the side showed its passage.

Afterwards the tracks were intermittent and eventually absent, suggesting the wagon had skipped and then turned end over end. But the wagon's eventual resting place was the unexpected one of being trapped at what was effectively the spout end of a funnel made by two slopes.

He ran his gaze along the top of the canyon, seeing nobody, then down the slope and the softer scree until it rested on the ground. A body lay a short distance away.

He winced and hurried on, but to his relief the body proved to be the guard's broken form. He had been thrown clear and then made his own way down.

Jim searched further away from the wagon, but he found no other bodies. But he did find footprints in the soft ground beside the creek.

There were two sets and they were heading upriver. This observation led him to pat his holster and find that his gun had been taken.

Cooper had survived and so had Emily, but clearly he had taken her hostage, then made good his escape.

If he were to follow them then rescue her, it would take a while to catch up with them and then move on to civilization. He would need provisions, so he spent the next half-hour clambering up to the wagon.

It proved to be too precariously placed for him to get on board, but he was able to see into all four corners and confirm that his belongings and provisions weren't there. From this position he had a panoramic view of the canyon and he consoled himself with the observation that his horses weren't visible.

Thankfully they hadn't fallen over the side, but with the scene of the wagon's demise providing him with no help, he set off walking upriver.

As far as he could tell they hadn't passed any places where Albright could get down to the canyon base, or at least not using a traditional, safe way. It was therefore likely that Albright would have to travel back along the canyon to Wilson's Crossing before starting to come up beside the creek. This was a journey of a day in each direction.

As the sun rose to cast light down the side of the canyon, he paced over the rough ground, running his gaze from the footprints he found whenever he crossed soft dirt to the sweep of the creek ahead.

If Cooper and Emily had left the wagon soon after it had crashed, they would have many hours on him, but equally they would have tired before long, and Emily was feisty enough to slow Cooper down. So he remained confident that he would catch up with them, but he caught no sign of them.

By the time the sun had poked above the canyon rim the ground had hardened and he'd lost the comforting sight of footprints.

When he judged that he'd walked for an hour, he stopped to rest and consider the terrain, but it remained as uninviting as ever. Without provisions he faced a difficult situation and it was one he could resolve only by catching up with his quarries. He glanced at the harsh sun, which was already making him slick with sweat.

With a snort to himself he decided that by the time the pursuing riders caught up with him he would be in no fit state to fight them off. His best chance was to turn back and meet them part-way, then throw himself on Albright's mercy.

The situation felt so unpromising

that he looked downriver and seriously considered the matter before he set off, walking on the same route as before. The best he could hope for from Albright was to be arrested for helping a prisoner to escape, but his group was unofficial, so the punishment could be worse.

He'd been walking for a minute when he registered what he'd seen while looking the other way. He stopped and wiped the sweat from his brow, muttering to himself to pull himself together; then he turned.

He'd been right. A trailing band of dust was rising a mile away. Riders were already catching up with him.

He looked along the barren sides of the canyon, but he saw nowhere where he could hide and have any degree of confidence that they wouldn't see him. His only hope was that they wouldn't be expecting to find him here. If he slipped down behind a rock and spread dust over himself, they might ride on by. But that wouldn't help Emily.

Albright was sure to treat her badly after she'd forced him to make this detour. So he stopped, planning to speak up for her.

The riders emerged from the dust, letting him see that only four men had made it down. They slowed as they came to the rocky area where Jim had sat, although they did look at him before attempting to traverse it.

Someone shouted out a barked order. A moment later a gunshot rang out. It kicked dust ten feet to Jim's right, but it had clearly not been just a warning shot.

Jim gestured at them with his arms raised, but a second shot tore out, this time clipping a rock five feet to his left. He backed away while still waving to show he meant no harm. But then the nearest rider came close enough for him to recognize him.

He wasn't from Albright's group. It was Pierre Dulaine.

Jim turned on his heel and ran, his gaze darting to the water and then up the sloping canyon sides, seeking somewhere to run to, but he saw no likely escape routes.

The creek was boulder-strewn and the raging water would dash him to pieces within seconds if he were to leap in, if he didn't drown first. The scree on the canyon sides led up to a sheer section that he'd never be able to climb even if he didn't have gun-toters taking pot shots at him from below.

Ahead the terrain didn't alter for as far as he could see. So with no hope in any direction he chose the only one that gave him a chance of prolonging the pursuit.

He fingered his shark's tooth, then veered away from the water and ran for the slope. With his legs pounding he reached the start of the scree and immediately slowed to a lumbering pace as he struggled to gain height.

His feet dug into the dirt and for every three paces he climbed, he slid back for two. But he consoled himself with the thought that as he was struggling, his pursuers would too, provided he could get out of their firing range.

He redoubled his efforts, getting some height as he worked his way up on a diagonal path. With every pace that he fought upwards, he expected lead in the back, but he trudged on for fifty paces without mishap.

He looked down. Pierre and his riders had crossed the rocky section and were now turning their attention on him.

'You have nowhere to run to, Monsieur Dragon,' Pierre called, his voice echoing in the canyon. 'Come down and we can talk this through.'

Jim continued to climb, judging he'd get out of range in another minute. He was now halfway to the start of the sheer stretch of rock and further along there was a narrow, dark recess where perhaps he might find a route up. It felt a small hope, but it was the only one he had and so he clambered on.

A slug whined off a rock two feet to

his side and a second shot skittered along beside his right foot, so close that he raised his foot to check he hadn't been hit.

'All right,' he shouted down. 'I give up.'

He paced round on the spot, noting the recess was around fifty paces away, then looked down with his hands raised.

'Come down,' Pierre shouted, pointing at the ground. 'I'm sure we can come to an arrangement that won't result in someone finding your bones out here in a thousand years.'

'We both like to win, don't we?' Jim said. 'But I've always thought we'd both do better if we worked together. There's me and my hunting skills, and you and your firepower. We'd make a great team.'

'I wouldn't go that far. I like beating you too much.'

Jim resisted the urge to shout back that this had yet to happen. He was too intent on catching his breath and he could only do that if he didn't annoy Pierre. He took a steady pace backwards, then another.

'I don't reckon either of us will win out here. This quest has become too complicated.' He backed away again.

'I don't care about your latest mission. I'm still concerned about the bones you got by me the last time. And stop backing away!'

Jim took another pace backwards; then, on seeing the men below raise their guns he turned on his heel and ran for his life. The brief break had rekindled his strength and, better still, the ground higher up was firm and he made quicker progress.

He pounded along almost as quickly as if he were on the ground. Lead pinged off rocks, but it wasn't as close as it had been further down. Pierre shouted at him, but he ignored him as, for the first time, he started to hope he might live to reach the recess.

Closer to, he saw that the gap in the sheer rock face had several large boulders at the entrance, lying half-buried in the scree. He put his head down and hurried on. A bullet kicked off the boulder in front of him. Then he reached the boulders and leapt up on the nearest.

There was soft ground beyond, so he dropped to his knees and skidded down behind it while turning, coming to rest with his chest pressed to the rock. He took deep breaths to calm himself, then looked up.

The recess was only ten feet wide, but it went into the canyon side for some distance. The sides were slick, suggesting water had exploited a fault, and that gave him hope that there might be a way to the top.

Keeping his head down he moved to slip into the recess. Movement sounded behind him. He started to turn, but then he stilled when a voice he didn't recognize muttered into his ear.

'Don't move,' the man said, backing up his order with the press of cold steel into his neck. 'You've got some explaining to do.'

8

The captured man raised his hands then turned to face them.

Despite the gun that Nathaniel had trained on him he gave a wide and disarming smile, then gestured with his head towards the men who were shooting at him.

'So,' he said, 'are you going to shoot me or are you letting them do it?'

'That depends on what you've done wrong,' Nathaniel said.

The man looked Nathaniel and Shackleton up and down with a quick flick of the eyes, clearly trying to work out whether he'd seen them before, so as to tailor his answer.

'Detailing everything I've done wrong would take too long, but if you're only concerned with recently, I wasn't responsible for what happened back there.'

Shackleton moved forward to consider him, his gun also drawn.

'So you were part of the lynch mob?' he asked.

The man rocked his head from side to side.

'Not exactly, but I'd guess that that question means you were the men the lynch mob were chasing.'

When Shackleton nodded, the man introduced himself as Jim Dragon and when the name failed to get a reaction he relaxed and leaned back against the boulder.

'What happened?' Nathaniel asked.

'I wanted Cooper Metcalf too, but not to hang him. This woman was with me, Emily Chambers. She wanted to question him about her father's disappearance. When she saw that Deputy Albright planned to lynch him, she took pity on him. She stole my wagon with him on board and raced down the side of the canyon, but it went over the side.'

'We saw some of that. Where are they now?'

Jim pointed upriver. 'Somehow the three of us survived the fall, but Cooper kidnapped Emily and they left me behind. I was following them when those men decided to use me for target practice.'

Nathaniel liked it that Jim hadn't withheld information to negotiate his way out of the situation; he glanced at Shackleton, who narrowed his eyes with a look that said he'd had the same thought. In a coordinated move both men lowered their guns, making Jim sigh with relief.

'And did these men follow you down?'

'No. They had a problem with me before I got involved with trying to free a man from a lynch mob.'

His continued honesty removed the last of Nathaniel's concerns, so he leaned on the boulder beside him, then raised himself to glance down at the scene below.

One man had stayed at the bottom of the scree while the other three were plodding up to them, clearly having been given unwelcome orders to flush Jim out.

The nearest man saw Nathaniel. He swung up his gun and loosed off a quick shot, but by then Nathaniel had ducked down out of view.

'Yeah,' Nathaniel said, 'they don't seem particularly friendly.'

As Jim nodded, Shackleton raised himself.

'You men,' he shouted, 'Jim's caught up with his friends. We've got no argument with you, so turn back and this ends here.'

'Pierre Dulaine won't listen to sense,' Jim said, 'but I'm obliged you tried.'

From beyond the boulders muttered comments sounded. Then someone relayed Shackleton's offer to Pierre. Silence reigned as they awaited an answer. It came when grit moved, the footfalls getting closer.

'They're still attacking,' Shackleton said.

He gestured to Nathaniel to move to

a higher position so they could get different angles on the men. Jim followed Nathaniel and shuffled down to sit behind him.

Slowly Nathaniel raised himself, so that he could see more of the scree, but now the men had moved away from the position they'd last been in. He continued to move up, letting him see the area immediately beyond the boulders, but still the men weren't visible.

Pierre was too far away to present a danger, but he waved at the gunmen, encouraging them to launch an attack. His directions unwittingly revealed where the gunmen had gone.

'They've slipped round to the bottom,' Nathaniel said, swirling round to face that way as a man appeared around the side of the boulder.

Shackleton had already reacted. On the turn he caught the man with a low shot to the guts that made him fold over and land at his feet.

A second man followed him, but

Nathaniel dispatched him with a high shot to the chest. The man dropped his gun before he keeled over to hit the boulder, then roll down it to the ground.

That left just the one man who had climbed up, but long moments passed without him daring to show himself.

Shackleton and Nathaniel exchanged glances that asked whether the other had heard anything, but all was silent. Nathaniel looked down to the bottom where Pierre was staring pensively at their position.

'There,' Jim said, pointing.

A gun was rising over the boulder between them; the man on the other side was planning to fire indiscriminately in the hope of getting a lucky shot.

Nathaniel used the same tactic. He pressed his chest to the boulder, stretched out his arm and fired down towards the man's position. He'd fired twice before the man jerked back his arm without firing. On the third shot a cry of pain sounded.

Nathaniel and Shackleton both jumped up, their guns swinging down to pick out the man, but by now he was rolling away from them.

He didn't try to stop his progress and he rolled down in a spreading cloud of dust until he flopped on to his back at the bottom. Pierre rushed over to check on him, then looked up.

He loosed off a gunshot that winged into the canyon wall ten feet above their heads, the shot appearing to be more in anger than to continue the attack. Then, before Nathaniel and Shackleton could repay the compliment, he hurried to his horse and beat a hasty retreat, heading back downriver.

They watched him flee until they were sure he wasn't planning to return. Then they checked on the other men, but they were all dead.

These were the first men they'd had to kill during the year that Nathaniel had worked for Shackleton, and then it hadn't been to defend their prisoner.

So they were in sober moods as they stood beside the creek and discussed their next actions, although their moods lightened when Jim rounded up the dead men's horses. Then he pointed out the tracks beside the water.

'Cooper and Emily?' Nathaniel asked.

'I hope so,' Jim said. 'I've been following them all day.'

Nathaniel looked upriver, seeing no sign of anyone.

Jim could be wrong, but as Albright and his group had gone downriver, heading upriver was the way Cooper would probably have gone. Besides, on horseback they would soon catch up with whoever had made the tracks.

Shackleton agreed with him so, before they mounted up, they both faced Jim.

'Welcome to the group,' Shackleton said. 'Let's hope we don't have to ride together for long.'

*   *   *

The house was a makeshift construction, having been built by placing logs that had drifted downriver over a circular arrangement of boulders. It was the first man-made feature in the unremitting terrain of the creek and the stark rocky sides that Jim had seen since he had joined up with his new companions two hours ago.

'Did you know this was here?' Jim asked.

'No, but usually we don't stray close to the sides along this section,' Nathaniel said. He looked up to the top of the canyon. 'And besides I don't reckon we could see it from up there.'

'Which could be why it was built here,' Shackleton said, peering at the house.

They had been following the tracks, seeing them only when they passed over the soft ground by the creek. They hadn't seen them for the last mile, but that might be because their quarries had veered away to the house.

'I'll check it out,' Jim said, dismounting.

'You'll stay here,' Nathaniel said. 'The prisoner is our responsibility.'

Jim smiled. 'He is, but he escaped, and that makes him as much my responsibility as yours.'

Nathaniel still dismounted leaving Shackleton to offer the sensible compromise.

'I'll keep lookout,' he said. 'Nathaniel, search the house. Jim, look for any sign of them having been here.'

With this plan Jim and Nathaniel paced towards the house until they were thirty feet away.

It was quiet, with no hint that anyone was within, and as they came closer, gaps in the wood let them see parts of the deserted interior. With more confidence in his stride Nathaniel headed on to the house while Jim moved past it, although he stopped when Nathaniel reached the door.

He watched Nathaniel look down through a gap in the logs then peer inside. Nathaniel emerged to shake his head, then disappeared from view as he began searching.

Jim began his own search. Soft dirt was between the rocks, but he found no tracks. However, when he swung further afield he found something that troubled him, even if it wasn't connected with the current situation.

Two cairns of rocks were set fifty feet from the house. Jim paced round to stand over them, but he found no markings to suggest who these people had been.

He must have looked at them, pondering for a while, as when he turned away Shackleton and Nathaniel had joined him. They were both looking through a collection of faded journals, which Nathaniel reported he'd found in a saddlebag in the house.

'That's all you found?' Jim asked.

'There was nothing else, and nothing to suggest anyone had stopped here in a while.'

Jim joined them in looking at the

papers. Several books had been torn in two and several others were bent over as if someone had tried to tear them apart but had failed. Nathaniel had put these in a pile to concentrate on the only intact one. It was filled with pages of notes written in a looping precise style that would take a while to read through.

While Nathaniel flicked through looking for anything interesting, Jim knelt to consider the torn up pages. He fitted the two halves of the book together then turned them over together.

Again, neat handwriting filled every page, although it looked as if it had been written by a different person from the one who'd written the other book. He was about to turn to the next journal when at the back he found two interesting larger pages, which had been folded then slotted into the journal.

He laid the sections together and peered at them intently, nodding to himself. Presently the other two caught on that he'd found something.

'Maps,' Shackleton said. He picked up the first. 'And it's of the Beaver Ridge area.'

Jim smiled. He hadn't worked that out, but he had figured out the other interesting fact. He pointed at the Beaver Ridge map.

'This square here is obviously what interested the maker, as the second map expands that area.'

Nathaniel and Shackleton took in the detailed squiggles that marked out the terrain. As he had done, they both noticed the numbers that had been dotted around. Then they attempted to read the key at the side that described what the numbers represented.

'Is this English?' Nathaniel said after three unsuccessful attempts.

'Nope,' Jim said, proud of his knowledge, even if it had come without any effort on his part while he'd been collecting money at the end of his missions. 'It's Latin, and those are the names of lizards.'

'They're no lizards I've ever seen.'

'And you won't. These are dragons.' He waited until both men stared at him. Then he shook his head and let the more sober aspect of this discovery overcome him. 'Perhaps not, but the map details the location of some very old and very valuable bones.'

'Made by the man you and Emily were searching for?'

'No. Emily said Cooper Metcalf had found a map, presumably this one, and that's why her father Seymour had come here. Cooper then led him up into the canyon, but he never returned.' Jim glanced at the nearest cairn, feeling unwilling to suggest the obvious next action. 'But if that grave says the search for Seymour ends here, the search for Emily and the bones continues.'

'I'm not sure it is Seymour,' Shackleton said as he joined the others in pacing around the rocks. 'If Cooper killed him, I don't reckon he'd bury him in such a noticeable place.'

'You could be right,' Nathaniel said,

'but either way, whose body is buried under the second cairn?'

'It'll take a while,' Shackleton said, 'to get Sheriff Bryce up here to investigate. So I reckon we need to learn all we can.'

They quickly allocated tasks and this time nobody complained when Jim volunteered to dismantle the cairns. Over the years his bone hunts had often acted on poor information that had led not to old lizard bones but to the more recently deceased.

So while the other two men read the journals in more detail, he moved rocks aside carefully so that he could replace them easily.

It took him ten minutes to find the dried-out body of an older man. Emily had provided no description, but it increased the possibility that this was her father. Then he moved on to the second body, and when he'd uncovered that, he stepped back in shock.

The body was a woman's. The skin had collapsed before drying, but she appeared to be young.

He was still thinking of possible reasons for this unexpected discovery when Nathaniel joined him. He had stuck a finger in one of the journals, highlighting a page that had interested him. His pensive expression said that what he'd found wouldn't please Jim, and that expression became more grave when he saw what Jim had uncovered.

'This section confirms who they are,' Nathaniel said.

'Go on,' Jim said when Nathaniel had remained silent for several seconds.

'As you thought, it's Seymour Chambers.' Nathaniel took a deep breath. 'He wrote this journal and it records how he travelled up here searching for old bones with a young woman.'

Jim knelt down beside the body.

'It's sad to get this confirmation. When we rescue Emily, she'll be pleased. But then I'll have to tell her that her father's dead along with a woman he probably cared for . . . ' Jim trailed off on seeing that Nathaniel was shaking his head. 'What's wrong?'

'It's the identity of the woman.' Nathaniel pointed. 'Seymour came here with his daughter, Emily. I reckon you've found her body.'

9

'Who was the woman who told me she was Emily, then?' Jim said, not for the first time. They were leading their horses down to the creek to resume their pursuit of Cooper and a woman whose identity had now become unclear.

'There's no reason for any deception that I can see,' Nathaniel said. 'So perhaps we got it wrong. Perhaps her father met up with a young woman and . . .'

Nathaniel trailed off. This explanation didn't sound plausible to his own ears and it was unlikely to satisfy Jim.

'I suggest,' Shackleton said, 'we stop worrying about the things we can't change and concentrate on the one thing we can: finding these people we've been tracking.'

Both men nodded, so they mounted

up and resumed the journey upriver. They quickly came across more tracks where the two people had crossed soft ground and, in a more positive frame of mind, they carried on.

Even if their quarries had abandoned Jim shortly after the wagon had crashed and then walked for the rest of the night, they shouldn't be too much further ahead of riders who were managing a mile-eating pace. But when they reached the next vantage point, a mile further on, where they could see around a long sweep of the canyon, there was still no sign of movement ahead.

The tracks beyond the house had been the last they'd seen and the dirt here was loose. They searched around, but found no signs of the two people's passage.

Unless they'd gone high up the canyon sides or into the water, they should have left tracks. Nathaniel cast his mind back and then nodded to himself.

'You two carry on,' he said. 'I'll shout if I'm right.'

He didn't wait to answer the inevitable questions; instead he turned his horse around and trotted back towards the house.

When he located the previous set of tracks he jumped down from his horse and stood beside them. He noticed that despite his comment Shackleton and Jim were returning at a steady pace. So, hoping that his hunch was right, he examined the prints.

They appeared to have been made by a man's boot and a smaller, presumably woman's, boot. He looked back along the line of footprints and they maintained a straight line until they stopped at the next rocky area, but there was something odd about them.

He could think of only one way to help him work out what was wrong. He walked along for a few strides, and then turned. Walking with a determined tread, as he'd expect Cooper to have done, he paced along beside the footprints. Then he returned and compared the tracks.

His footfalls were different. They were fresher and so crisper, but it wasn't just that.

He knelt, pondering while the other two men came closer, leaning forward in the saddle with curiosity about what he'd found. When they pulled up, he had a theory.

'We've been duped,' he said. 'We were meant to follow these tracks and keep on following their route even after they stopped appearing.'

'You mean Cooper and this woman didn't make them?' Shackleton asked.

'No. It's them all right, but they tried to be clever. They walked backwards.'

Shackleton and Jim both furrowed their brows, but when they'd jumped down to see what Nathaniel had noticed they reached the same conclusion as he had. The footfalls were different from Nathaniel's, with the heels making only a slight mark, as if they were walking with their weight set on their toes, or as Nathaniel now surmised, walking backwards.

As it was probable that Emily hadn't been kidnapped and that these two had perhaps even helped each other, it wouldn't have been hard for them to avoid the soft patches of dirt. But they hadn't, and that had been deliberate.

They'd walked on them to create a trail before missing a patch. Then they'd walked backwards over this section of soft earth to give the impression they were still moving on while in fact they'd doubled back and hidden somewhere.

'Where would they go?' Jim said, looking downriver. 'The terrain's so stark we'd have seen them.'

'It is,' Shackleton said. 'But they only needed to hide while we passed.'

'And,' Nathaniel said, 'I reckon I know where they've gone.'

Shackleton and Jim swung round to look at him, but when he said no more Shackleton glanced away while he considered, then gave a slow nod. Jim nodded a few moments later.

'Clever,' they both said.

★ ★ ★

Jim slipped closer to the edge.

On the other side of the gully Nathaniel was matching his movements, while Shackleton guarded the entrance. They had ridden hard to get here.

Their quarries' bluff had been to double back to the place where he had met up with Shackleton and Nathaniel. Then they had climbed out of the canyon.

From there, afoot, the only place where they could hole up quickly was the gully in which they'd stayed last night, a place where nobody would expect them to go.

If Nathaniel's hunch proved to be wrong they didn't have an alternative plan.

Jim caught Nathaniel's eye in the low light and gave him a supportive smile.

Then they peered over the edge, as the men who had captured Cooper last night would have done.

At first Jim could see nothing in the dark below, but after a minute he detected movement, then he heard a whispered comment. He couldn't hear the words but they had been spoken by the woman who had called herself Emily.

He gestured to Nathaniel, who fingered the rope at his side. Nathaniel had joked earlier about how it would be fitting to recapture Cooper in the same way as he'd been taken, but now it was too dark to try that.

They settled for using the safe manner, which didn't require Jim to do anything but keep lookout in case of unexpected developments.

Nathaniel made his way down to join Shackleton. Five minutes later Jim caught a glimpse of Shackleton moving through the entrance. Of Nathaniel he saw no sign until a sharp cry of alarm sounded.

'It's over, Cooper,' Nathaniel snapped. 'Don't move a muscle or we deliver a dead man to jail.'

Rapid footfalls sounded before the woman shouted out.

'Get off him. I'm armed and I will shoot.'

'You're not armed. Cooper has your only gun.'

A grunt of irritation echoed in the gully before footfalls hurried towards the entrance. A brief scuffle sounded. Then Shackleton's heavy footfalls moved on.

'It was a good try,' he said. 'But now there'll be no more mistakes.'

'Everything about this is one big mistake,' the woman muttered, her tone aggrieved but resigned.

'Save your breath,' Nathaniel said. 'Although there's one person here who'd like to hear your explanation.'

As it was unlikely that there'd be any surprises now, Jim reckoned this was his cue to come down.

When he entered the gully his vision

had adapted and he could see the outlines of the four people within. They would be moving on quickly, but while Nathaniel secured Cooper, there was enough time for questions.

'Who are you?' Jim asked.

The woman lowered her head, so Shackleton gave her an encouraging nudge. He was holding her arms but he hadn't tied her up.

'I'm sorry,' she said, not looking at him. 'I didn't want you to find out this way. I'm Flora.'

'And getting dashed to pieces at the bottom of the canyon was a better way, was it?'

'I didn't know that it would be the only way I could free Cooper.' She looked up. 'He's my brother. I had to help him. You can understand that, can't you?'

Jim sighed, then gestured to Shackleton to release her. While Shackleton helped Nathaniel finish tying up their prisoner, Jim sat beside her. After a moment's thought she sat.

'I can,' he said. 'No matter what Cooper's done wrong, you'd want to help him.'

'But that's just it,' she implored, leaning towards him. Her watering eyes caught a stray beam of light. 'He didn't kill Narcissa and neither did Washington Cody kill Mayor Maxwell.'

'Except that, based on what we saw back at that house, the real Emily Chambers and her father met Cooper and paid with their lives.'

'Don't waste your breath,' Cooper snapped before Flora could respond. 'These men won't listen to reason.'

Flora stayed quiet; it looked as if she wouldn't say anything more, but when Nathaniel moved to escort Cooper out of the gully, she raised a hand.

'Wait,' she said. 'I need to explain. You're all good men and there has to be a way out of this.'

'Go on,' Jim said, although Nathaniel and Shackleton grunted unenthusiastically.

'Washington Cody used to stay in

that house when he fished. My brother went there once. He wasn't interested in fishing, so he explored. He found an old journal and a map. He made enquiries that led him to Seymour Chambers. They exchanged letters and they even mentioned you as an expert. Eventually Seymour and his daughter came out to see him.'

She looked at Cooper, who shook his head, seemingly refusing the offer to take up the story, but then in a rush he blurted out the details.

'I led them up the canyon to the house. They were alive when Sheriff Bryce arrived to arrest me,' he said. 'I left willingly, thinking it was all a big mistake, but someone must have killed them later. Then I found that Washington had been found guilty of killing Mayor Maxwell and it's all gone badly wrong since then.'

'For you and Washington it has,' Shackleton said levelly.

'Washington would never kill anyone and neither would I,' Cooper muttered.

He took a deep breath. 'I wrote to Flora telling her what had happened. But by the time she arrived I was next in line to spend the rest of my life in Beaver Ridge jail on a ridiculous charge.'

'You're wasting your time telling us this,' Shackleton said.

'I know. You men haven't got the guts to make a stand against injustice. You'll never do the right thing.'

'But we are doing the right thing. We deliver prisoners to jail. That's our job.'

'Even when the prisoners you deliver are innocent?'

'They're all innocent, if we were to listen to their prattling, which we don't.'

Cooper shook his head sadly. 'Then you'll be taking a lot more innocent men to jail now that Deputy Albright has got his claws into Bear Creek.'

Shackleton sighed. 'I know you've got good reason to hate him but, misguided though he was, he was after you because he wanted to know what you did with Narcissa's body.'

139

'I did nothing,' Cooper spluttered. 'The last time I saw her was a week before she was killed.'

'And that's the problem,' Nathaniel said. 'It's not our duty to work out if you're telling the truth. So we can't do nothing to help you.'

'You two might not,' Flora said as Cooper lowered his head showing he'd finally run out of patience, 'but I hope Jim might still do something.'

'Me?' Jim murmured with an incredulous tap of a finger against his chest. 'What can I do?'

She turned to him. 'I hired you because you have a knack of uncovering the truth, no matter how well buried. I still hope you can do that. Even if there's nothing I can do to stop these men taking Cooper to jail, his innocence can still be proved.'

Jim tipped back his hat. 'That's beyond my abilities. I find the bones of long-dead lizards, and that's still the only result I want out of this unfortunate situation.'

Flora glared at him, her upper lip curled in a look of disgust, before she turned away.

'I can see that now,' she said, then stood.

Everyone reverted to silence as they left the gully to go in search of somewhere to spend the night that was more open, and which could be readily defended if Albright came.

In the dark it took them two hours to clamber back down into the canyon and reach their horses. When they moved out, Cooper walked between Nathaniel and Shackleton and Jim let Flora ride while he walked behind Cooper.

She didn't acknowledge his gesture.

They'd moved on for another hour before they discussed where they would stop. Neither man consulted Jim as he looked back down the canyon.

It was too dark to see anything other than the outline of the canyon and that was only noticeable because it concealed the stars. But he could hear distant sounds which, when he strained his hearing, proved to be people calling to each other.

The sounds were miles away, but they were down in the canyon. And they sounded animated and angry.

'Deputy Albright,' he said.

10

'They're gaining on us,' Shackleton said, his urgent comment making Nathaniel look over his shoulder.

Sadly he was right. A dozen men were on the trail with others spreading out to either side seeking to outflank them. As they had five people and three horses with Cooper riding with Nathaniel and Flora sitting behind Jim, their pursuers should be able to reach them within the next mile.

Their situation was precarious and it was doubly annoying, as yesterday they had been successfully staying one step ahead of Albright.

After a pensive first night spent guarding their recaptured prisoner, while listening to the sounds that Albright's distant camp was making, they'd set off several hours before first light. They alternated walking duties, although they ensured that Flora rode most of the time. When the light came they'd caught no sight of the pursuit and nor did they hear it for the rest of the day. But they had no doubt they were being followed, and worse, there was only one route along Devil's Canyon.

The next day they'd set off early again, and as they'd emerged from Devil's Canyon to begin the trek to Beaver Ridge, the panoramic view back down the canyon revealed that Albright had sneaked closer during the night. He was only five miles behind them and during the day he'd closed that gap.

Now, with the distant town visible in the early afternoon heat haze he had chosen his moment to swoop.

'We'll reach the ridge before we get to the town,' Nathaniel called. 'We could find somewhere to hole up there.'

Shackleton didn't reply immediately, showing he was unwilling to try this last resort.

'All right,' he said at last, with a

reluctant slap of a hand against his thigh. 'There's a pass through to Beaver Ridge ahead. We'll make our stand there.'

Nathaniel didn't know the area well enough to know of this pass, so he drew back slightly to let Shackleton take the lead. With a destination in mind, the riders gathered a last burst of speed from their tiring mounts. They even gained some distance from their pursuers before Shackleton veered to the side and headed to the ridge.

Nathaniel couldn't see where they were aiming for until they were fifty yards from the ridge and a thin gap opened up in the rocks. Large sentinel boulders were at the entrance and Shackleton swung wide to make towards them.

Jim hollered a warning to slow down, but Shackleton kept going. It wasn't until they were within seconds of reaching the boulders that Nathaniel saw that the pass swung away behind the left-hand sentinel before cutting into the ridge.

In single file they surged through a pass that was so thin it wouldn't let them ride side by side. They weaved to the left and right between sheer rock walls before Shackleton slowed.

He waved back at the others with a downward gesture that told them to prepare to dismount. They had to do this in short order as, when they emerged from the stretch of sheer walls, the terrain ahead sloped upwards steeply towards the top of the ridge. It would be a hard, slow climb of several hundred feet and they would have to lead their horses while being visible as easy targets from below.

With escape not possible for the moment, Shackleton applied himself to the more pressing problem first. He gestured around, giving his orders silently.

Nathaniel rushed to the left of the entrance while Jim moved to the right. They both positioned their charges where they could watch them while still looking to the entrance, leaving

Shackleton the freedom to roam.

Shackleton slipped down behind a boulder facing the entrance; then they waited for the first person to risk showing himself. Long minutes passed during which time the clop of hoofs stopped fifty yards back from the entrance. Then shouting sounded as the pursuers considered their tactics.

As Albright had not mounted an immediate assault Nathaniel looked around the terrain. Unlike the place where they'd been ambushed two days ago, nobody could approach them unseen; the only effective option for an attack was between the two sheer rocky walls.

Albright's superior numbers meant he could overrun them easily if he came in force, but the lack of cover meant they could make him pay a heavy toll. Their best hope lay in Albright's forces not being as committed as they'd appeared.

For the next fifteen minutes that possibility appeared as if it might be realized as Albright's men stayed out of sight. So Nathaniel started planning the journey down the other side of the ridge and then to Beaver Ridge. They would need to cover several miles over rough terrain, but if they were to attempt it now they might be able to cover some distance before Albright dared to make his assault.

That thought made Nathaniel wonder how Albright could be sure they hadn't done that immediately.

'He must be able to see us,' he said to himself, and although his quick consideration of the terrain failed to reveal any likely hiding-spots he called out to Shackleton.

'You could be right,' Shackleton said, raising himself to look down the gap between the rock walls and then around the pass.

Shackleton flinched a moment before a gunshot tore out. It echoed in the narrow pass, making it hard for Nathaniel to work out where it had come from, but Shackleton took no chances: he dived into cover. On the other side of the entrance Jim also ducked down, but then bobbed back up in a different position. With steady assurance he sighted a spot fifteen feet up the side of the entrance.

Jim fired two rapid shots. After the second shot he was rewarded with a screech closely followed by a thud as a body fell to the ground.

Nathaniel looked up. Now he saw the ledge to his side along which the man must have crawled. The dark rock made its extent hard to discern and he moved backwards while running his gaze along the fault.

Another shot rang out to his side, making him look that way, but then from the corner of his eye he caught a flash of colour and jerked back. A man was leaping down from the ledge. Nathaniel swung round to face him, but he was already too late. The man slammed into his chest, throwing him on to his back.

Nathaniel lay stunned with the man

lying on top of him. The man's glazed eyes and stillness showed that the drop had also stunned him. Weakly Nathaniel pushed him away and the two men rolled to the side. Then Nathaniel tried to rise, but his limbs were still jarred and he struggled to right himself.

His assailant didn't have as much trouble as Nathaniel had, and he delivered a backhanded swipe to Nathaniel's jaw that knocked him aside. Worse, Nathaniel's gun went skittering away. Nathaniel watched it come to rest, shook his head to rekindle his battered senses, then flexed his shoulders in readiness for making a dive for it, but the man had already turned his gun on him.

Nathaniel stared down the barrel of the gun, seeing the man's eyes widen as he prepared to fire. But then a hollow thud sounded and the man flinched. His gun dropped from his hand.

For a moment Nathaniel thought Shackleton or Jim had saved him, but then the man keeled over, to reveal Cooper kneeling behind him. His arms were raised showing he'd sneaked up on the man, then delivered a scything blow to the back of his head with his manacles.

Cooper watched the man until he came to rest. Then he leapt at his dropped gun, gathering it up with speed.

'I saved your life, Nathaniel,' Cooper said, levelling the gun on him. 'Don't make me take it.'

Nathaniel moved up to a kneeling position and spread his hands, getting into a position where he could go for his own gun, which lay five feet to his side. He glanced around. Shackleton was out of view and Jim and Flora were having an altercation of their own: Flora was attempting to come to Cooper's aid and Jim was holding her back.

He saw no sign of any more of Albright's men sneaking up on them, but if they were, this was an opportune moment to attack.

'You won't get far,' Nathaniel said.

'We're trapped.'

'I have a gun, and that gives me and Flora a chance.'

'An escaped prisoner who's as notorious as you are won't avoid justice.' He glanced at Flora who had now fought herself clear of Jim and was hurrying across the entrance to the pass. 'And your sister will be in as much danger as you are. If you care about her, take your punishment.'

'How can I take my punishment when I'm an innocent man?'

'And how can I believe that when you have a gun on me?'

Cooper winced, providing Nathaniel with some comfort that he wouldn't fire. Nathaniel stood and with Flora running on at a pace that would reach him within seconds he took a long pace towards Cooper with his hand held out.

'Stay back,' Cooper said.

'Prove you're an innocent man and hand over the gun.'

'I can't do that. Don't force me, Nathaniel.'

Nathaniel took another pace as Flora swung round towards with them with Jim at her heels. Her hurried arrival made Cooper glance at her and, taking advantage of the sudden distraction, Nathaniel rushed forward. With his attention elsewhere Cooper backed away for a pace, but then he stumbled on the loose ground, going to one knee. By the time he'd righted himself Nathaniel was on him.

He slapped both hands on his wrist pushing the gun down, then bore down to press him to the ground. Flora screeched as the escape attempt took a bad turn. Scuffling feet sounded, presumably as Jim caught up with her.

Nathaniel put them from his mind and concentrated on the gun. His tight grip made Cooper drop the weapon. Then he gripped Cooper's shoulders and upper arms firmly.

Cooper struggled, but his recent rough treatment had weakened him and his endeavours were ineffective. Without too much trouble Nathaniel dragged him to his feet to find that Jim had secured Flora in the same manner. Shackleton, though, was glaring past them at the entrance, as if he expected Albright to mount another attack at any moment.

'You should have taken your chance,' Flora said, struggling but finding that Jim's grip was resolute.

'I couldn't,' Cooper murmured. 'I'm not a killer.'

'Then there's no way out for any of us,' she said.

Since both he and Jim had to watch out for their charges seeing that they were trapped miles out of Beaver Ridge, Nathaniel had to agree. He looked at Jim, hoping for a word of encouragement, to find that Jim was smiling.

Jim went over to Cooper's hat, which had come loose during their scuffle. He picked it up. Then, with a wink to Nathaniel, he removed his own hat and placed Cooper's hat on his head.

'I have an idea,' he said, shrugging out of his jacket.

'I am not doing this,' Flora said, digging in her heels.

'You don't have a choice,' Jim said. 'This is the only way your brother will get to live.'

He pushed her up the slope. She paced on for another few paces before she stopped and slammed her hands on her hips.

'You saw what happened back there. Cooper could have killed Nathaniel, but he didn't. How can you help Nathaniel and Shackleton take him to jail after that?'

'He stumbled. If he hadn't, I don't know whether he'd have fired or not.'

She sneered. 'When I hired you I thought you were a decent man.'

'I thought you hired me because you knew I wasn't.'

Flora shook her head, but since Jim offered her no option she turned and continued climbing. They were heading up the side of the pass with the sheer stretch of rock to the right and the top of the ridge to the left.

As Jim had observed during his earlier consideration of the terrain, ahead the slope became shallower. Then their route skirted along the top of the pass and back down on to the plains. They should come out some distance away from where Albright should be planning his assault, but not so far away that his plan wouldn't work.

When they swung away towards the pass Jim looked down at the three men who had stayed behind. Nathaniel nodded to him then, along with Shackleton, he blasted a burst of gunfire into the air. The two men waited for a moment, then fired twice more. Then they ducked down behind cover.

They had done the most that they could. Jim turned away and he and Flora worked their way across the rough terrain. When the downward slope came into view it was as passable as he'd remembered, but there wasn't much cover to keep them hidden from anyone who was looking their way.

Flora slouched along, making no attempt to seek cover. Jim didn't stop her. Being seen was, after all, his plan.

They were halfway down to the bottom when he first saw a group of men by the entrance to the pass. The sight broke Flora out of her fugue. She looked around, forlornly seeking an alternate route before she hurried down into a gap between two rocks.

The men below caught the movement and started pointing. Jim dallied ensuring he was seen, then joined her in her hiding-place.

'And now what?' Flora grumbled, folding her arms.

'We wait for Albright to capture us.'

'And then shoot us up?'

'It could happen, but we'll have a better chance than we had holed up back there.' He offered her a smile she didn't return. 'And that's what I always do. Take the one option that might work.'

She snorted at the unlikely possibility of his plan working, then looked away from him, letting Jim give his shark's tooth a quick rub without her seeing it.

'Then you'd better change out of my brother's jacket or they might hang you instead,' she said.

Jim gulped, accepting this was likely. Then he waited with as much composure as he could muster for Albright to come for them. He didn't have to wait long. Rustling sounded down the slope, then came muttered orders.

'Your escape attempt failed,' Albright called. 'Come out and you'll live for long enough to swing.'

Jim sighed with relief as he got confirmation that Albright had divided his forces. Then, with a murmured comment to Flora to stay down, he raised his hands and stood.

He saw that Albright and another seven men had taken the bait.

'I hope you won't do that,' Jim said lightly. 'We'd prefer it if you'd let us get away from all the shooting back there.'

Albright opened and closed his mouth soundlessly as he looked Jim up and down, taking in the clothing he'd swapped with Cooper. Behind him at the pass entrance shooting exploded as Nathaniel and Shackleton made their bolt for freedom with their prisoner. Now they had the advantage of one man for each horse.

'I'll make you regret this,' Albright muttered before he turned on his heel and directed his men to hurry back down the slope.

11

'You don't look pleased,' Shackleton said when Nathaniel joined him at the bar.

'Some jobs make you feel satisfied,' Nathaniel said. 'Some don't.'

Shackleton poured him a whiskey, then topped up his own glass. He waved the bottle at Jim, but he was reading one of the journals and he placed a hand over his glass.

'Did you see the governor?'

Nathaniel snorted, then leaned on the bar beside Shackleton. With one hand he cradled his glass and with the other he withdrew an envelope and tossed it on the bar.

'Yup. All my troubles are over, apparently.'

While Shackleton opened the envelope and read the contents, he downed his whiskey, then poured another.

Although Nathaniel felt bitter now, he'd been elated when Jim's plan had worked. They had stayed one step ahead of Albright, who had given up the chase before they'd reached the prison gates.

They'd handed over Cooper, reporting as always that they'd had a quiet journey. Then they'd located Jim and Flora at the arranged meeting point. They had been safe, although the rescue hadn't pleased Flora. They'd left her and Jim in town, then, while Shackleton had returned to the prison to receive their new orders, Nathaniel had seen the governor.

'He's recommended to Judge Matthews that he should declare you a free man,' Shackleton said, handing back the envelope. 'So, now that you've served your year working for me, what do you want to do next?'

'The same as before, I guess,' Nathaniel said, tapping the envelope against his other hand.

Shackleton considered his sombre

expression with a gleam in his eye.

'I preferred you when you weren't free.'

Nathaniel ignored the attempt to make him lighten his mood and took a last glance at the letter. The governor had congratulated him on completing a year without mishap, proving that he was a changed man. Perhaps he was, but that didn't mean he had to like the changes.

'I did too,' he grumbled, tucking the envelope away.

Shackleton considered him with a smile playing on his lips, then leaned closer.

'It's time you had the lecture again, the one you didn't like having when you first joined me.'

'I remember it.' Nathaniel uttered a heavy sigh. 'Don't get involved.'

'And why is that no longer keeping you content?'

Nathaniel fingered his glass before he took a long sip.

'In my time I've been a deputy

sheriff, a bounty hunter, an outlaw, a prisoner, and now I'm a guard, but in all that time I've never accepted that I should just do what I'm told without question.' Nathaniel turned to Shackleton. 'I reckon we've delivered two innocent men to jail and that means something rotten is going on back in Bear Creek.'

'You could be right, so it's a good job for us that our next job is in Monotony. We leave in two days to pick up — '

'A new job doesn't help. Our duties will eventually take us round to escorting more prisoners from Bear Creek, and what then?'

'Nothing. If the prisoners have been duly found guilty, it's not for us to decide they're innocent and let them go, is it?'

Nathaniel sighed and hunched over his drink.

'I know, but . . . '

Shackleton hunched over his drink too and lowered his voice to a sympathetic tone.

'Cooper may have saved your life, but then again he was trying to escape. If you carry on dwelling on that, do you know what you'll become?'

'What?'

'Deputy Albright.' Shackleton waited until Nathaniel winced before he continued. 'He got so involved in the case that he became obsessed with finding Narcissa's body. That made him abandon his duty and try to lynch Cooper.'

'It did,' Nathaniel murmured, the hint of an idea about how he would resolve his concerns coming to him. 'He pursued that aim beyond all reason.'

'He did, but you're a better man than he is, so you can put aside such thoughts.'

'I'll try.'

Shackleton patted his back, then took a gulp of his drink.

'Now don't go thinking that I've not had the same thoughts. But in the end the only thing you can rely on is that you treat everyone the same and you let someone else make the tough decisions on the rights and wrongs. Unless you can come up with a better way, I suggest you do the same.'

As Shackleton moved aside to give him time to ponder, Nathaniel returned a brief smile, acknowledging that he'd snap out of his ill mood soon, but even so, one thing was certain: he'd done his duty by delivering the prisoner. Now that Cooper was locked away and safe from Albright's lynch mob he was free to uncover the truth, no matter how long it took.

So far he had only one potential line of enquiry that might lead to the truth: Narcissa's undiscovered body. He didn't know how that'd help when Judge Matthews had already deemed the evidence against Cooper to be strong enough without a body, but it had interested Albright, so it might be a possible way to start.

With this positive thinking cheering him, he edged along the bar to see what was intriguing Jim so much that he didn't want a refill. When Jim noticed his interest he turned the maps he'd found in the journals round for him to see.

'You know Beaver Ridge better than I do,' he said, pointing at a marked square, 'where do you reckon this area is?'

To take his mind off his problems, Nathaniel studied the map. The outline of the canyon at the bottom helped him to work out which area it covered, and the ridge that overlooked Beaver Ridge was marked giving him a broad feeling of where the square would be. But it didn't help that the map was so old that even the town wasn't marked.

'The square is where you reckon these lizard bones will be?'

'Yeah,' Jim said, waving the second map. 'Someone found them long ago and then drew this map detailing the bones' location, except it doesn't help when I don't know where the area is.'

'And Seymour's journals don't help?'

'No. The only entries I've found

suggest he and Cooper hadn't worked it out either.'

'And yet whoever killed Seymour tried to destroy his journals.' Nathaniel considered. 'I wonder if finding these bones will help Washington and Cooper.'

'I can't see how it can.' Jim shrugged. 'Although as we don't know why Seymour was killed, I suppose it could help. It certainly can't hinder them.'

'And do you reckon they're innocent?'

Jim sighed. 'I spent a week with Emily . . . Flora . . . and until I found out that she'd helped Cooper to escape I thought her a good woman. Now that I've got used to the truth, perhaps I still think that.'

Nathaniel looked again at the map. Around the square that was blown up in more detail on the other sheet, there was a dotted line, which elsewhere indicated a depression. There were no large depressions of this kind in the area, except one . . .

Nathaniel shook his head, trying to

dismiss the idea, but it seemed the only possibility. He traced a finger along the various outlines helping him to picture the scene. Slowly he looked up at Jim and smiled.

'Those tales you told on the way here about your exploits. Are they true?'

'Of course.'

'Even the ones concerning your trick of spiriting away items in the false bottoms of wagons?'

'It's my speciality.'

'In that case I know where your bones are.'

* * *

'I'm a busy man,' Governor Bradbury said, 'so be quick.'

Jim gave a nervous smile as he shuffled up to the desk, while ignoring the winks that the two guards who had escorted him to the governor's office were making to warn the governor about what was to come. Jim had already surmised that the only reason they'd let him come here was to have a laugh at his expense, but he didn't mind as it had got him an audience with the only man who could help him.

'I have a great favour to ask,' Jim said, then removed his hat and turned it over in his hands, 'and it's one that will greatly aid science and our understanding of the world.'

Bradbury's gaze flicked to the grinning guards. He sniffed then leaned back in his chair.

'I'm always prepared to help people understand the world better. Tell me what's on your mind.'

'Dragons,' Jim said with a gleam in his eye that he didn't have to feign. He waited until a smile played at the corners of Bradbury's mouth before continuing. 'Your quarry doesn't just contain rocks for your prisoners to smash. It contains the bones of long-dead lizards.'

The guards leaned forward in anticipation, but to their surprise, and Jim's,

Bradbury disappointed them.

'It does.'

Jim flinched back. 'You mean you already know about them?'

Bradbury shrugged. 'I didn't know they were dragon bones until now, but my predecessor noted how from time to time these large bones appeared. He didn't know what they were, so he threw them aside.'

'A pity,' Jim said. He rooted in his pocket for the map, which he laid out on the desk. 'But luckily I have a map that was made before the prison walls went up. It pinpoints where all the bones are.'

Bradbury gave the map a cursory glance. 'And I assume you want to dig up the rest?'

'I do.' Jim gave a hopeful smile.

Bradbury waved at the piles of paperwork on his desk.

'I'll think about it.'

He lowered his head, showing that this meeting was over, so Jim coughed, making the governor look up, coldness

170

replacing the previous hint of interest in his eyes.

'I'd prefer an immediate answer. I have the map and my tools. I can get digging and get those bones out of your way quickly.'

'Why the hurry? You said these dragons have been long dead, so they're not going anywhere.'

The guard to his left grunted a laugh as at last the governor mocked him.

'I know, but I'm in a hurry.' Jim sighed and rocked from foot to foot. 'I've already made promises to deliver these valuable bones to the people who want to study them.'

'Valuable, you say?'

Jim frowned, as if this element didn't concern him, even though it was the one word he had hoped Bradbury would notice.

The next ten minutes went as well as Jim's negotiations usually did.

Bradbury came out of it smiling, having struck a bargain that would keep Jim and the guards assigned to keep an eye on him happy. Although it wouldn't satisfy him if he discovered how much Jim's contacts were prepared to pay for the bones.

While Jim was counting out the dollars on to the desk and Bradbury was at his most vulnerable, in a casual voice he mentioned the most important matter behind his visit.

'There's one other thing,' he said. 'I need help in translating the map.'

'These two will help.'

Jim paused from his counting to consider the guards, then shook his head.

'I need expert help. And you have two new prisoners who met the only man who knew all the map's secrets.'

Suspicion narrowed Bradbury's eyes, so Jim leaned away from the bills he'd already counted out. He cast a significant glance at the ones in his hand.

The next ten minutes went more easily than the first half of the negotiation had.

172

Neither party disguised their true feelings. Bradbury identified Jim as being someone who didn't care about the bones other than for the money he could make from them, and Jim identified Bradbury as someone who put money before the welfare of his prisoners.

When the bribe was carefully stored away in Bradbury's pocket, Jim was led out of the office and down through the prison to the wall that surrounded the quarry. From there Jim watched the milling prisoners and guards, who at first presented a chaotic scene, but it was one which gradually showed itself to have order.

Guards looked on at each group of prisoners, who were engaged in their pointless task of smashing rocks. Other guards stood further back supervising several groups while the guards on the top of the wall oversaw everything.

All the guards were attentive and they took delight in goading their prisoners on for even the slightest deviance from their rock-breaking routine. Anyone seeking escape would have numerous layers of authority to get past and that was before they faced the double wall around the quarry and prison.

When Jim had drunk in his fill of the scene, he used the map to orient himself. He soon worked out that the bones were in an area in which the prisoners weren't working, making his task easier. However, the pitted nature of the ground there suggested that, aside from the bones that had been dug up, he would struggle to find any more.

He waited for half an hour until a guard came over from the main bulk of workers with a prisoner in tow. Jim assumed he was Washington Cody. In a co-ordinated move another guard emerged through the gates to the prison with Cooper Metcalf.

When they'd led them to the barren area, Jim was escorted down to the quarry, where he skirted around the edge to join the other men.

Cooper and Washington were casting

odd glances at each other; both men were probably wondering whether this unexpected excursion to an unused part of the prison would turn out badly. But they were nodding to each other, this being the first time they had met since parting at Wilson's Crossing.

Jim kept his eyes wide, attempting to convey silently the urgency of the situation. So, when Cooper first caught sight of him, he merely gazed at him.

'Let me introduce myself,' Jim said, speaking up before Cooper could show that he knew him. 'I'm Jim Dragon and I want to use the information you learnt from a very special map.'

'I don't know nothing about no map,' Cooper said, furrowing his brow and still maintaining the surly and uncooperative attitude he'd adopted after they'd caught him in the gully.

'I know that neither of you knows who I am,' Jim said, speaking quickly to cover up how much he was labouring the point. 'But I do know you can help me and I'm sure you don't want to disappoint your guards.'

Washington's wince confirmed that he knew the consequences of disappointing a guard, and in the silence Cooper spoke up.

'In that case I'm sure we can help you,' he said. 'I reckon I've seen that map before.'

His cautious answer confirmed he'd understood the charade Jim was playing, so Jim smiled, then gestured ahead at the rocks.

'Then I'll explain what we can do,' he said, 'to make life easier for us all.'

12

'Go well?' Nathaniel asked when Jim joined him in the saloon.

'A lot better than I feared,' Jim said. He went on to relate his exploits in the jail that afternoon.

'How long will it take?'

'Only another day. There's nothing left for me to find. They'd already dug up all the bones and piled them at the side of the quarry. So I'm spending my time trying to make it appear that Washington and Cooper are helping me.'

Nathaniel nodded. 'I'm obliged you're taking the risk.'

'No problem.' Jim looked around. 'And Shackleton, does he accept the risk?'

Nathaniel sighed and hunched over his drink. He didn't want to speak ill of his trusted partner, but he hadn't been enthused about Nathaniel's taking direct action, so rather than risk an argument Nathaniel hadn't told him what he was up to.

'He's supported everything I've told him,' he said.

Jim considered him, but he didn't press the issue, and the two men turned to debating the fine points of the next day's plan.

An hour later Nathaniel and Jim had covered the details from every angle they could think of. So, after thanking Jim again for his help, he left him to head back to the hotel where he and Shackleton were staying.

Outside, darkness was descending and few people were about, a late fall chill hurrying them on their way. He paced down the side of the road that let him see the jail beyond the edge of town. He couldn't help but imagine what it was like for Cooper huddled up in a cell after being convicted for a crime he knew nothing about.

Convinced now that he was doing the

right thing he turned to the door, but then stopped as from out of the shadows figures emerged.

Two men came from around the left-hand side of the hotel; two more men came from the right while from across the road more shadowy figures made their way towards him.

Nathaniel considered them, then hurried on to the door, but Deputy Albright stepped out of the doorway and into a patch of light. He leaned back against the jamb with a confident smile on his face.

'You were deep in thought,' he said. 'Were you congratulating yourself on having beaten me?'

'Nobody beat anybody,' Nathaniel said with a weary tone. 'In the end everybody did their duty, something we can all continue to do now that Cooper Metcalf is where he should be.'

Albright sneered, suggesting he wouldn't take up Nathaniel's offer to end this matter.

'Except some people did more than

they needed to do.'

Nathaniel lowered his head and stared at the hardpan for several moments. Then he paced up on to the boardwalk to face Albright.

The other men tensed and when he glanced over his shoulder, he saw that at least ten men were spreading out to surround him.

'We're the same, Albright. We have a duty to perform and whether we agree with it or not, we complete that duty. I've been tempted to act when I don't agree with the decisions others have made, and you've been more than tempted, but in the end we just do the best we can.'

'Fine words, Nathaniel McBain, but you've gone too far. We could have got on well, but when you side with men like Cooper Metcalf, there's no hope.' Albright sneered. 'But this isn't over. I have friends in the jail. They'll get the answers I want out of Cooper.'

Nathaniel spread his hands, still seeking common ground.

'You're determined to find out what happened to Narcissa, but trying to capture Cooper before he reached the jail wasn't the answer. Having someone deal with him in jail isn't the answer either.'

'That's the difference between us, Nathaniel. You did what you had to do, but you roam from place to place. You have no ties. I go further because I care about my town.' Albright gestured around him. 'And so do these men.'

Nathaniel turned, and took in the ring of men around him.

'There's not so many of them now. From what Jim said, fifty men left Bear Creek, all fired up and ready for a lynching. Now there's a dozen. Perhaps you haven't got as much support for your form of justice as you claim.'

'Or perhaps I have the same level of support as I've always had.'

Nathaniel judged that his answer meant these men had always been sympathetic to Albright's viewpoint and the others had been just the usual

181

hangers-on who got involved whenever there was trouble.

He decided further talk would serve no purpose. He moved to walk past Albright into the hotel, but the deputy stepped to the side to block his way.

'Move aside, Albright,' Nathaniel muttered. 'We have nothing left to say to each other.'

'We don't, but we're not finished yet. I reckon it's time Governor Bradbury hired some new people.' Albright snorted a laugh. 'Now that the old ones are no longer able to carry out their duty.'

'Is that a threat?' Nathaniel said, although the firm footfalls around him provided the answer along with the distinctive sounds of at least three guns being cocked.

'It's an order. I've had enough of your meddling, so give up your job and stay out my sight. Then this'll end here. Do anything else and you won't live for long enough to draw another breath.'

'You don't order me around, Deputy Albright.'

Nathaniel flexed his shoulders ready to move quickly as he fought for his life, but a new voice spoke up.

'Like he said, you don't give the orders, Albright.'

Nathaniel looked to the left to see that Shackleton was standing behind the circle of men, with a gun trained on them.

A second set of heavy footfalls sounded from the right and Jim Dragon stepped into view to level a gun on the men from the other side.

'An interesting stand-off,' Albright said. He stood upright in the doorway, but he kept his confident expression. 'Three men against twelve. I know who I'd back to survive.'

Nathaniel conceded this point with a shrug.

'Even if you prevail, Marshal Conrad runs a peaceful town here. He'll make you pay for this.'

'The marshal is out of town and he won't be back in Beaver Ridge for a week. He can't help you and in my experience, lawmen tend to believe the survivors.' Albright settled his stance. 'Time to see who gets to tell his side of the story, Nathaniel.'

Nathaniel matched Albright's action, his hand drifting towards his holster. In his mind he rehearsed the action of drawing his gun while leaping to the side.

The outcome would depend on how many of his opponents Jim and Shackleton were able to dispatch in the initial onslaught. But then he stayed his hand.

A rifle barrel poked out through the open doorway and jabbed into the side of Albright's neck. The deputy flinched, then jerked his head to the side to see Flora walk out on to the boardwalk.

'The only certain thing,' she said, 'is that that man won't be you.'

Albright gulped, his darting eyes displaying uncertainty for the first time.

'Why have you sided with them? They took the man you were trying to free to prison.'

'I don't have to answer your questions. Just raise those hands or I'll let you have it.'

'In that case . . . ' Albright glared at her, making Nathaniel think he'd defy her threat, but then slowly he raised his hands.

'Now,' Flora said, flashing a glance around the circle of men, 'you will all leave town one at a time. The moment the last man leaves, I take this rifle off Albright.'

Albright pointed at the nearest man, who followed his silent order.

Then one at a time the rest of the men peeled away. Several went to the saloon for their horses, the rest to the stables. Five minutes later a line of men was riding out of town.

None of them looked their way again, but they rode at a deliberately slow pace. As promised, when the last man reached the edge of town Flora lowered her rifle.

Albright mockingly tipped his hat to her, favouring her with a long stare, then moved off. He stopped beside Nathaniel.

'This doesn't end here,' he said, looking straight ahead. 'Your next duty takes you out of town. It'll be your last duty, as you won't reach Monotony.'

He paced off the boardwalk and headed to his horse. Like the other men he didn't look back at the group that had gathered outside the hotel.

When he'd disappeared from view Nathaniel thanked the others, ending with Flora.

'Obliged,' he said. 'But like Albright, I'm surprised you stepped in.'

'I surprised myself,' she said. She glanced at Jim. 'But after the trouble I caused I owed you all.'

'You did,' Shackleton said. He came over to the hotel doorway. 'But keep your door locked tonight and be careful. Albright won't forget this.'

'Neither will I,' she said, lowering the rifle to her side.

Shackleton nodded, then patted her shoulder before glancing at Nathaniel.

'Does this mean you've changed your mind?' Nathaniel asked.

'I'm still not getting involved,' Shackleton said. He rubbed his jaw. 'Unless Albright gets in my way.'

He winked. That being the extent of the help Nathaniel had wanted, he headed into the hotel. Nathaniel checked that Albright was still moving off into the night, then followed Shackleton, but Jim loitered at the back, clearly still bemused at Flora's sudden change of mind.

'What's the real reason you helped?' he asked when they were all in the hotel lobby.

She laughed while considering Nathaniel, the sound welcome after the many hours during which she'd favoured them with her stern mood.

'I guess the truth is I hated you as much as I hated Albright, but now I accept you were just doing your duty while he was abandoning his. That means that once you'd completed your duty, you're free to do the right thing.'

187

'I don't know what you mean,' Nathaniel said levelly.

She lowered her voice. 'I know you're planning to break Cooper and Washington out of jail.'

Nathaniel narrowed his eyes. 'What makes you think that?'

'I saw the wagon Jim bought yesterday. He's having it altered to include his speciality, the feature that helped him get a cargo of bones past Pierre Dulaine.'

Nathaniel winced, lost for words, leaving Jim to speak up.

'I suppose the big question now is,' he said, 'if you've worked that out, will Governor Bradbury?'

13

The loading of the bones was proceeding quickly.

Jim had accepted that the map was useless. It merely noted the positions where the bones had been before the prisoners had dug them up and then tossed them aside.

Luckily they had been piled up to the side of the quarry, so Jim had been able to box them up. Few were intact and most were smashed so badly even he took a while to confirm that they were in fact bones. But he'd dug up bones that had been in a worse state than these and the people who would pay him were used to putting them back together.

His failure to use the map didn't stop him consulting Cooper and Washington, who now understood what was expected of them. So they played along studying the map, providing sage advice, and then pacing out across the quarry as they sought out the locations indicated by the various symbols.

This section of the quarry was the furthest from the walls and so the most secure, so the guards didn't interfere; instead they stood back to watch proceedings.

It was early afternoon when all the crates were filled and it was time for the final action of loading them on to his wagon. Nobody had paid the wagon as much attention as Flora had yesterday.

Jim signified to the guards that he was ready. They allocated him another eight prisoners to manoeuvre the heavy crates on to the back of the wagon. From the corner of his eye Jim caught a gradual movement along the tops of the walls as more guards moved into position to watch the process.

When most of the crates were loaded, Governor Bradbury arrived to stand by the gates. Jim studiously avoiding looking at him. But Bradbury did ensure that the crates were loaded carefully while providing plenty of unneeded advice and directions.

Despite the governor's hindrance, after an hour Jim's wagon was loaded up and the guards signified that the prisoners should stand back to let him leave.

Jim carried out this part of the process quickly. Then, with a quick fingering of his lucky shark's tooth, he set his gaze on the gates 150 yards ahead and moved his horses on around the perimeter of the walls.

Behind him he heard the guards collecting the prisoners to take them back to the main quarry. He gritted his teeth, knowing what was about to come, but still finding that he was more nervous than he usually was when trying one of his old tricks.

On the previous occasions only his own skin had been at stake, but this time other people were relying on him.

He had halved the distance to the gates when the first cry of alarm went up. He kept his gaze set forward and carried on at the same measured pace.

Bradbury was already moving in front of the gate to intercept him, but the noise from behind drew his attention. He gestured to the nearest guards, ordering them to find out what was causing the growing commotion.

Jim did his best to pretend he couldn't hear the commotion and hailed Bradbury.

'Thank you,' he called out, 'I collected more bones than I feared I would. Your men and your prisoners are to be commended for their help.'

With his hat raised and a cheery smile on his lips he swung the horses round to approach the gates. They remained resolutely closed, so he had no choice but to pull up beside Bradbury.

Bradbury raised a hand, signifying that he should remain seated. 'Spare me your fast talking,' he muttered.

Jim raised himself in the seat to consider the closed gate. Then he looked around the quarry, eventually settling his gaze on the area that he'd just left. Guards were moving to quell a disturbance and with consternation rippling through the prisoners, more guards were surrounding each group and ordering them to quieten.

'If there's going to be trouble back there,' Jim said, 'I'd welcome being allowed to go through the gates while you deal with it.'

'Nobody goes anywhere when there's trouble, least of all you.'

As the guards Bradbury had dispatched were hurrying back with their expressions thunderous, Jim reckoned this was a good time to be silent. He looked straight ahead while putting on an innocent smile.

The guards gesticulated and muttered to Bradbury, who grunted back orders to them, after which they stepped back for a pace and glared up at him with their arms folded. In the quarry the prisoners were being lined up and counted. Bradbury's burning gaze made Jim look down.

'I will be able to leave with my bones,' Jim said, 'won't I?'

'I doubt you will ever be able to leave, and I look forward to the many years you'll be here as my guest.'

'I don't understand. Whatever is going on back there has nothing to do with me.'

'Two prisoners have gone missing: Cooper Metcalf and Washington Cody, the two men who were helping you.'

'That has nothing to . . . ' Jim trailed off when he saw a new man making his way down from the wall, someone he hadn't seen since the gunfight in Devil's Canyon.

'I believe you know Pierre Dulaine,' Bradbury said.

'I've met him,' Jim muttered. 'And I'm sorry you had to suffer his company. That man would sell his own children for a quick dollar.'

Bradbury chuckled as Pierre joined him. 'Then I reckon you two ought to become friends.'

'That'll never happen,' Pierre said. He licked his lips as he struggled to avoid smirking. 'Monsieur Dragon reckoned he'd bested me before, but now it's time for him to get what he deserves and for me to get what I'm owed.'

'The bones are yours,' Bradbury said, 'as we agreed, but first I want my prisoners back.'

He gestured to the guards who jumped up on to the back of the wagon. Jim swirled round on his seat to watch them tap the base of the wagon.

'You are not giving this man my bones,' he muttered.

'You'll be lucky,' Bradbury muttered, 'if I stop with your old bones. After helping prisoners escape, I might fillet you.'

As Pierre laughed at Bradbury's wit, Jim watched the guards patter back and forth searching for a way to get into the false bottom. The access point was well hidden and they would need to remove most of the crates to reach the plank that could be raised.

They took the more direct route.

Another guard came over and threw them a pickaxe and a crowbar, which they then proceeded to use to tear apart the base. Jim protested, but nobody listened to him as Bradbury and Pierre edged forward to peer over the side of the wagon and monitor progress.

When they'd broken away a wide enough section to look down, one man stood back while the other knelt and peered into the revealed space. He looked from side to side then rocked back on his haunches.

'Nothing,' he said.

'Don't be fooled,' Pierre said. 'This one hides the obvious in plain sight.'

With an exasperated sigh the guard slipped through the gap and out of view. Grunting sounded, marking the exertion required and the occasional bruised limb gathered in the tight space. Presently he emerged and shook his head again.

'I've been into all the corners,' he

said. 'There's nothing down there.'

Bradbury shot Pierre a harsh glare, but he was unmoved.

'I should have realized Monsieur Dragon wouldn't try exactly the same trick twice,' he said. 'I checked the crates the last time because I didn't know the bones were in the false bottom. This time he'll have hidden them in the crates.'

'The only thing in the crates is the bones everyone saw go in there,' Jim protested, standing up and putting his hands on his hips.

'I've had enough of you,' Bradbury muttered as the guards got to work on the crates. He signified that Jim should jump down, then faced him with the third guard at his shoulder. 'I've heard thousands of versions of the innocent act from prisoners. Yours is even more unconvincing than most.'

'I'll take that as a compliment,' Jim said, 'although I should say — '

He didn't complete his retort when the guard stepped in and delivered a short-armed jab to his side that doubled him over. He staggered round on the spot, then grabbed the side of the wagon to steady himself. He drew himself upright, but that only let him face the governor's glaring face.

'This is the worst escape attempt I've ever seen,' he muttered.

'But it isn't,' Jim gasped as the guard drew back his fist. He scrambled into his pocket and withdrew the map. 'I'm just a bone hunter using this old map to find more bones.'

The second blow was a backhanded swipe that sent him spinning along the side of the wagon. He grabbed hold of the end to stop himself falling, and stood there, gathering his breath and looking at the quarry.

'That's yet to be proved,' Bradbury said.

'If this map won't prove it, what will?' Jim asked brightening as his gaze picked out two men from the mass of gathered prisoners.

'The sight of Washington Cody and

Cooper Metcalf will do it.'

Jim raised a defiant arm then pointed while swirling round to face Bradbury, the sudden movement making his battered ribs protest.

'Then look over there, you fool.'

Bradbury's eyes flared at the insult and he moved in ready to deliver the next blow himself, but the guard cried out.

'Look!' he shouted. 'He's right. The prisoners are over there.'

Bradbury flinched. Then, with Pierre, he looked towards the quarry where the guards had isolated the men they had been looking for. Another guard was hurrying over to report the news.

'A diversion?' Bradbury muttered and when Jim answered with only a smile he gestured up at the men on the wagon. 'Keep looking. There's still two prisoners missing.'

'Just don't move the bones far,' Jim said, rubbing his ribs ruefully. 'It'll take you a long time to put them back in.'

Bradbury muttered to himself, then

swung round to meet the oncoming guard, who slowed to a reluctant walking pace before he reached him, his slouched posture showing that he was the bearer of news that wouldn't please the governor.

'Everyone is accounted for,' he reported. 'Nobody's missing.'

'But I was told two prisoners had escaped, and that they were Cooper and Washington.'

'They must have gone back into the main quarry before they were ordered to move. We got it wrong.'

'You can't have,' Pierre said, stepping forward. 'Monsieur Dragon came here to break prisoners out of jail in the false bottom of his wagon.'

'Except I didn't,' Jim said, not having to feign his hurt feelings, 'and I'd welcome being allowed to leave now.'

'You can,' Bradbury said with a dismissive wave of the hand as he turned to Pierre. 'But you can't. You have some explaining to do.'

Jim waved the map at Pierre, smiling,

before Bradbury and the guard surrounded him. Jim jumped up on the seat. One guard stayed on the back to replace the lids to the crates while the other stepped over into the seat to signify ahead that the gates should be opened.

'Sorry,' he said as Jim got the wagon moving forward.

'You weren't to know who to trust,' Jim said as they passed through the gate.

'I can see that now. But Pierre Dulaine sounded convincing when he told the governor you were hiding something.'

Jim sighed then folded the map up and slipped it back into his pocket.

'Pierre Dulaine has come to believe,' he said, 'that I'm a man who hides secrets away in plain sight.'

14

'Did it work?' Nathaniel asked when Jim Dragon drew his wagon to a halt beside them.

'Of course,' Jim said as he jumped down. 'It was one of my greatest triumphs that will — '

'Spare me the details and tell me what you got,' Shackleton said as Flora squealed with delight and hurried to the wagon.

She dropped to her knees and sought out a knothole on the side.

'Get them out first,' she said. 'They must be suffocating in there.'

'If anyone were down there,' Jim said, 'they'd have plenty of air, but I'm afraid that nobody's in the false bottom.'

'But,' she murmured, swirling round to face them, 'you said you were getting them out.'

Jim smiled. '*You* said I was getting

202

them out, something that Pierre Dulaine was also so convinced I was doing he gave me an ideal diversion.'

Flora looked from one man to the next, noting that they were all smiling, before stamping a foot.

'Someone had better explain what's going on here before I give you what Deputy Albright nearly got.'

Nathaniel nudged Jim forward.

'Go on,' he said. 'Stop funning her.'

Jim reached into his pocket and withdrew the map of the jail.

'We decided to get them out the proper way,' he said. 'The guards searched me every time I left, but luckily this time everyone was so convinced I was smuggling out prisoners, they didn't realize it was just the map I was getting out.'

She cast the map a disdainful glare.

'You forget. That doesn't interest me. I'm not the bone enthusiast's daughter I said I was.'

'I remembered, but the map that'll interest you is on the other side.' Jim turned the sheet of paper over to reveal a new drawing.

Nathaniel and Shackleton moved over to consider it. Bold lines clearly indicated the entrance to Devil's Canyon at Wilson's Crossing. The reason for the fainter lines was less obvious, and Nathaniel looked up for an explanation, but Jim was still trying to placate Flora with a side smile.

'I don't understand,' she said. 'What's so interesting about the entrance to Devil's . . . ?'

She trailed off and looked aloft as the obvious thought hit her.

'For the last few days,' Nathaniel said, 'Deputy Albright pursued your brother with a determination to lynch him that made no sense when he'd already been sent to jail for life. He said he wanted to find out what Cooper had done with Narcissa's body, but maybe we misunderstood why he wanted that information.'

'Because,' Flora said, while nodding eagerly and moving round to see the map, 'what he really wanted was to ensure that nobody ever found it.'

'That's what I surmised. His real aim was to stop Cooper and Washington meeting up in jail and discussing what they'd seen that night. Perhaps they both saw something separately that they didn't understand at the time that showed where the body was.'

'So,' Jim said, finishing the explanation, 'I got the two men together, and when the guards weren't paying attention they compared their stories. On the night Mayor Maxwell was killed, they were in different places, but they both saw a group of riders heading into Devil's Canyon. These lines show where those men went. It's a wide area, but a bone-hunter like me should be able to find her.'

Flora nodded. 'Are you sure that finding her body will help to prove Cooper's innocence?'

'No,' Nathaniel said. 'But Albright didn't want anyone to find her, so her body must lead to the real culprit. I'd guess that man is Albright. And I reckon he also went up into Devil's Canyon and killed Seymour Chambers and his daughter because they'd also seen the events of that night.'

'So we've worked it out,' Flora said, smiling for the first time since Jim had returned.

'We have,' Nathaniel said, blowing out his cheeks.

'Now all we have to do is to live for long enough to tell someone about it.'

* * *

Riders were on the trail ahead, blocking his route between two slopes.

Jim trundled the wagon on towards them, seeking to run them off the trail, but two men stood further up the right-hand slope and levelled rifles on him.

Jim slowed the horses and came to a halt ten feet from the riders.

'What's wrong?' he asked in a pleasant tone, although he couldn't help but touch his shark's tooth.

None of the men spoke. Then other men appeared from the scrub, all also gun-toting.

Jim recognized them as being the men who'd been in town with Albright. The deputy himself stepped out from behind a boulder to the left to look up at him.

'You is what's wrong,' he said.

Jim lowered the reins and put on a hurt expression.

'If you've talked to Pierre Dulaine, he was mistaken.' Jim paused for just long enough to see Albright wince, confirming that the deputy had met Dulaine. 'He'd got this mad idea into his head that I was helping prisoners escape.'

Albright craned his neck to see into the back of the wagon where the broken planks were piled up alongside several opened crates.

'Seems others had the same idea.'

'He convinced Governor Bradbury, but only Pierre would be stupid enough to fall for a trick like hiding people in the bottom of a wagon.'

'And what did you do with Pierre?'

'Nothing. The last I saw of him Bradbury's guards were taking out their irritation on him. I doubt I'll see him again.'

'An interesting story. And now you're just riding out of town with your bones?'

'Sure.' He gestured back towards Beaver Ridge. 'I know you have a problem with Nathaniel and Shackleton, but I suggest you resolve that with them. It has nothing to do with me.'

Jim raised the reins, but Albright swung his six-shooter to the side to pick him out, making the other men tense up.

'You are going nowhere,' Albright said. 'Get down off the wagon and explain yourself.'

Jim considered the various gunmen. He counted six, although he didn't doubt that the others who had been with Albright in town would be close by.

Seeing no other option, he jumped down from the seat and faced the deputy.

'I can't say any more. I was wrongly accused back in the jail and now I'm leaving town with the old bones I came to find.'

'Except I know that's not the real reason you went to Beaver Ridge jail.'

'I don't know what you mean.'

'You saw Cooper Metcalf and Washington Cody.'

'I did, but only to get them to help me with a map I didn't understand.'

'I don't care about no map. All I care about is that you met them. And people who talk to those two always meet unfortunate ends.'

Albright gestured and two men hurried to his side. They disarmed Jim, then grabbed one arm apiece.

'So you're going to kill me in cold blood just because I talked to two prisoners, are you?' Jim muttered, keeping his chin high.

'Not quite in cold blood. You and

that woman denied us a lynching.' Albright laughed. 'So I reckon we'll change that.'

Jim struggled, but the two men bundled him round the wagon to sit him in the back.

Albright joined them and sat on one of the crates that had survived the search at the jail. The other men sat on the base beside the broken planks with their feet resting on the false bottom.

Two of the men remounted their horses and a third man climbed on to the seat, then the wagon moved on.

'Where are you taking me?' Jim said after they'd trundled on for a hundred yards.

'I passed a tree a mile back. It looked tall enough to ring your scrawny neck.'

Jim gave another experimental shake of his shoulders, but the men holding him had a firm grip.

'You didn't get away with this the last time, and you won't get away with it this time.'

'But I will.' Albright craned his neck

to look around before his gaze fell back on Jim. 'There's nobody around who can stop me.'

Albright licked his lips, clearly relishing Jim's retort before he uttered it.

'What makes you think that?'

'Because we've learnt from our mistakes. There's only a half-dozen of us here. The others are still scouting around. They were following you along with Nathaniel, Shackleton and the woman. They saw you meet up beyond the ridge and talk. Then you headed off on your own, clearly planning to be a decoy again, to draw me out. Well, you've done that, except it hasn't worked as I already knew you were a decoy.'

Albright laughed, then glanced at the men holding Jim, encouraging them to laugh too. Jim waited until they had returned to silence, then fixed Albright with his confident gaze.

'I fooled a clever man like Pierre Dulaine twice,' he said. 'What makes you so certain I can't fool an idiot like you twice?'

15

'Nathaniel and Shackleton won't be able to help you,' Albright grunted. 'My men will keep them away from the hanging tree.'

'Splitting your forces was a bad idea when taking them on,' Jim said.

'You can't worry me. I have this area covered. There's no direction they can attack that'll take me by surprise.'

In the false bottom, lying beneath the crate on which Albright was sitting, Nathaniel looked at Shackleton and smiled. The strips of light slipping in through the side planks illuminated Shackleton's twinkling eyes, letting Nathaniel see that this comment had amused him too.

Flora was lying beneath the area where Jim was sitting, a position in which she dare not move for fear of Albright seeing her through the large gap in the wood. The two men hadn't been happy about her accompanying them on this mission, but she'd refused to listen to reason or to take their offer to make her own way back to Beaver Ridge with the map.

She'd argued that she was in as much danger on her own as she was with them. With time pressing, they'd agreed. And within the next few minutes they would find out if they were right.

The wagon was slowing, presumably as they reached the tree. Shackleton caught Nathaniel's eye, checking that he was ready to act. Nathaniel nodded, then moved his head until he could see through a gap in the side, confirming that the wagon was drawing up beside a large oak.

With a lurch the wagon halted. The riders who had accompanied them jumped down and a rustle sounded, presumably as Albright threw a rope to them.

Scuffing footfalls sounded as, through

the gaps between the planks, shadows darted from side to side. Jim was struggling to avoid the noose.

Nathaniel had hoped something might happen that would give them a better chance of success, but clearly that hope was fading fast. He gave a downwards gesture to Flora, backing up their agreement that no matter what happened next she was to stay down.

She had the map and if they were killed, she had to ensure that the truth got out.

The scuffling feet moved closer to Shackleton's position. With a raised hand Shackleton ordered Nathaniel to stay the attack for a moment. Then he rolled beneath them, not attempting to mask the noise he made and, lying on his back, he aimed his six-shooter up through the planks.

Four rapid shots blasted out, two for each man. He was rewarded with cries of pain followed by heavy thuds.

'Ambush,' Albright shouted, leaping to his feet.

'Where?' someone else shouted.

Nathaniel didn't give anyone enough time to work out the answer. He rolled twice to place himself under the gap in the planks. Then he sprang up.

The two men who had been holding Jim were lying sprawled on the base of the wagon while Jim was rushing to the nearest man to secure his gun. Albright was swirling round towards Nathaniel, his open-mouthed expression registering his surprise that the ambush wasn't coming from afar.

Nathaniel made him pay for his indecision and leapt at him. He grabbed his gun arm and thrust it high, the action dragging out an air shot. Then the two men tussled as Nathaniel walked Albright down the wagon.

Shackleton emerged with his head down. Bent over, he scurried to the sideboards, laid his gun hand on the top, and picked out the men who had swung the rope over a branch. Both men were staring up a rise, expecting that the gunfire had come from the cover of several nearby boulders.

Two crisp shots rang out, dispatching them.

As Nathaniel's and Albright's entangled progress reached the back of the wagon, Jim gathered up a gun. The driver was turning in his seat while raising himself to scramble for his own gun, but before he could fire Jim slammed lead into his side. The blow stood the man up straight, before a second shot sent him tumbling to the ground.

Heartened by their successes Nathaniel redoubled his efforts to subdue Albright and take him alive. They had the map and that might lead them to Narcissa's body, but Albright alive would be more useful in freeing Cooper than he would be if dead.

Nathaniel wished that that wasn't the case when he backed into a crate. The rim slammed into the backs of his knees and with a reflex reaction his legs buckled. He went down on his rump on the crate with Albright bearing down on him.

Slowly Albright got the upper hand, pressing him down against the wood until he was lying flat. Worse, the deputy was able to drag his arm down. The gun moved in towards Nathaniel's chest.

From the corner of his eye Nathaniel saw Jim and Shackleton turn to help him.

'I can deal with this one,' Nathaniel grunted. 'Keep lookout for the rest.'

The confident comment made Albright grunt with anger. He strained even harder to bring the gun in, but his concentrating all his attention on the gun gave Nathaniel enough room to drag out his other arm and deliver a short-arm jab into Albright's side.

The blow landed without much force, but it was enough to rock the deputy to the side. Still entangled, the two men rolled off the crate to slam to the bottom of the wagon.

They rolled twice, coming to a halt with Albright still on top. Disconcertingly the wagon had moved slightly and now the noose they'd made for Jim dangled overhead. The sight spurred Nathaniel on.

He braced his back against the wood, then kicked upwards, but his legs became caught up with Albright's and they merely rolled to the side, to fetch up against another crate.

With Nathaniel's back wedged into the corner, they glared at each other from a few inches apart. Albright's eyes were wide and angry, and worse, he now had a free hand to drag the gun round and aim it at Nathaniel's chest.

A shadow passed over them. Flora stepped into view.

Despite telling her to stay hidden, Nathaniel didn't mind her intervention when, with one well-placed foot, she trapped Albright's gun against the wagon floor. Then she kicked the gun away.

Confident now of success Nathaniel used the few moments while Albright clenched his hand to roll Albright on to his back. Then he drew himself up and with one hand placed on Albright's chest to hold him down he drew his gun. With a quick gesture he thrust it deep into the deputy's guts.

'If you kill me,' Albright muttered, 'you won't get away from here. You're surrounded.'

'We've halved your numbers with ease,' Nathaniel said. 'The rest won't stop us delivering you to justice.'

Albright shook his head, but he didn't reply. Nathaniel checked how the others were faring.

Shackleton and Jim had taken up positions on either side of the wagon, from where they were looking out for trouble. Flora had gathered up Albright's gun, so Nathaniel entrusted her with guarding their prisoner. Then he released his hold and fast-crawled along the wagon to join Shackleton.

'If the rest are out there,' Shackleton said, 'they're staying well hidden. I reckon we should head back to Beaver Ridge now.'

'They were searching for us, so they

could be some way away. We should give them a while longer for the shooting to draw them in.'

'I reckon it's more likely that they ran when they heard the shooting. All the time Albright's group has been reducing in numbers. I reckon these men here were his inner group, the ones who rode off that night to bury Narcissa.'

'You could be right,' Nathaniel said, getting up. But a bullet tore into the boards a foot to his side, making him drop back down. 'Or then again you could be wrong.'

Shackleton snorted a laugh, then concentrated on looking out for the attackers. But they didn't have to look far: a trailing line of men was coming down the rise.

They ran from boulder to boulder in an organized manner, shooting off covering fire as each man made for the next position. But there were only three men.

Nathaniel reckoned this confirmed Shackleton's observation that the remaining men weren't as committed as the inner group had been, and it was likely that the others they'd seen in Beaver Ridge had given up. Nathaniel resolved to make them pay for choosing the wrong man to back, but then found that his hope that they would lack motivation was unfounded.

Together all three men jumped up and laid down a sustained burst of gunfire that forced everyone in the wagon to drop down out of view.

Lead tore through the wood and for self-preservation Shackleton and Nathaniel rolled to the side to get away from it while Jim gave up on guarding his side of the wagon.

When the gunfire petered out Nathaniel looked up, but it was to see that the area was deserted. He was just looking for where the men had gone to ground when two men leapt up on to the back of the wagon. They vaulted the backboard and landed crouched down with their guns aimed up at them.

From ten feet away both men fired. One bullet winged into the top corner of a crate; the slight deflection it took was enough to whirl it past Nathaniel's right cheek so closely he was sure he heard it whine.

The other shot was for Shackleton. It flew wild. But before either man could shoot again their opponents had them in their sights.

Nathaniel fired high, hitting the man who had shot at him in the forehead and making him crumple, then topple over the side of the wagon without making a sound.

Shackleton fired low, slicing a shot into his assailant's side. The shock made him lose his balance and reel backwards into the backboard.

He righted himself but two more shots rang out, one from Shackleton, the other from Nathaniel. Both slugs tore into his chest. He jerked upright, clawing at his bloodied chest before tumbling from view.

Both men knelt, poised and ready

for the last man to make his move, but Jim reacted first. He hadn't been paying attention to the other two men and instead he was lying on his chest, listening. He fired down through the base of the wagon, grouping his shots.

On the third shot a cry of pain went up from below, but he fired twice more before looking up.

'He won't give us no more trouble,' he said.

'You sure have keen hearing,' Shackleton said.

'Not really. I had an access point put into the false bottom from underneath. It creaks.'

While Shackleton joined Jim in peering into the bottom of the wagon to check on the man, Nathaniel ran his gaze over the rise, but he couldn't see any more signs of trouble.

He was just starting to think that the crisis was over when Flora screeched. He swirled round to find that she was lying sprawled on her back.

'I'm sorry,' she said. 'I couldn't stop him.'

Nathaniel didn't reply, the sight of what Albright had done with his freedom shocking him into silence. Instead of running to safety, he'd leapt on a crate and had stuck his own head through the dangling noose.

'One step closer,' he muttered, glaring down at Nathaniel, 'and I jump off.'

'What kind of threat is that?' Nathaniel murmured, still surprised.

'It's a good one. You wanted me alive, so that's the only weapon I have.'

'Then jump. It'll save the law doing it in Bear Creek.'

'Maybe, but I've got nothing to lose, so you'll stop me if you want Cooper Metcalf freed.'

'We have all the details of what happened to Mayor Maxwell and his daughter. That'll be enough to get him freed.'

'Except that when Sheriff Bryce investigates and finds all these bodies of

Bear Creek folk along with my hung body, he'll draw his own conclusions.' Albright snorted a laugh. 'He doesn't like lynching.'

Nathaniel spread his hands. 'So what deal do you want here?'

'Back away off the wagon and keep on going. You make one wrong move and I kill myself and leave you with a nasty problem to explain. You stay in sight all the way back to the place where we caught Jim. Then I move on.'

'We'll come after you.'

'You will, except you have a duty in Monotony that you can't avoid, so I reckon I'll get to tell my story first.' He laughed. 'And I should have enough time to move a body.'

Nathaniel nodded, accepting that a lot could happen between here and Bear Creek. The others looked at him with raised eyebrows, but he signified that they should join him in jumping down from the wagon.

On the ground they looked up at Albright, standing with his feet placed wide on the crate, the noose tied tightly around his neck with the rope taut enough to force him to stand tall. Slowly they backed away.

'I reckon,' Shackleton whispered from the corner of his mouth, 'that I can shoot through the rope before he jumps.'

'Save it until you have to,' Nathaniel said.

'But we can't let him get away with such a ridiculous stunt.'

'We can't, but he's right. We want him alive and I can't think of a way out of this other than to do what he wants.'

Jim stopped walking and looked at them.

'Then maybe it's time for me to step in,' he said. He turned to Albright and raised his voice. 'Do you want to take some advice so as to avoid dying up there?'

'I just want you to keep walking away.'

'Except we don't want you to die just yet, so remember that the crate you're standing on is empty. The lid won't support your weight for long and you wouldn't want the crate to tip over and make you hang yourself accidentally. So keep standing on the rim and you'll be fine.'

Albright glared down at him, but Jim said nothing else and hurried on to join the others in backing away.

'I knocked into that crate,' Nathaniel said, 'and it was full of bones.'

'It is, but I've found that if you tell someone to avoid thinking of doing something, it'll be the only thing they can think about.'

Sure enough Albright shuffled his feet to keep them on the rim, but that made him shake. He moved again, but the shaking worsened. He tried to synchronize the movement of his feet to avoid tipping the crate, but he stumbled.

That movement was too great for Albright to keep his equilibrium and he slid off the crate with a pained cry of alarm. The rope drew taut as he swung from the noose, his feet clattering against the side of the crate as he sought to regain his footing.

Nathaniel raised his gun and sighted the rope, but Shackleton laid a hand on his wrist and pushed the gun down.

'Wait,' he said. 'The drop didn't break his neck. Let him enjoy the fate he wanted to inflict on Cooper.'

Nathaniel bit back his distaste at seeing a man hang and instead he watched Albright's increasingly weak attempts to place a foot on the crate.

'How long?' he said.

'I reckon another . . . ' Shackleton raised a hand then slowly counted down with his fingers. 'Now!'

He drew his gun and while walking forward the two men blasted lead at the rope. It took four shots to hit the rope and another two to leave it with a single cord that stretched then broke, depositing Albright on the base.

Then Nathaniel joined the others in hurrying to the wagon to secure the deputy in preparation for a longer, legal session with the rope.

16

'Sheriff Bryce reckons that'll prove it,' Jim said when he emerged from the law office.

Flora looked aloft for a moment, breathing deeply to calm herself, before she offered Jim a big smile.

'How long before Cooper and Washington are freed?'

'They were tried and found guilty, so it could take a while. But Judge Matthews has said he'll look on the case favourably, and apparently he doesn't make such statements unless he means it.'

'Then I guess I'll have to be patient.'

She paced back and forth twice, demonstrating that she would be unlikely to take her own advice. Jim could already envisage her hounding Sheriff Bryce and the judge several times a day until they freed Cooper and Washington.

In that she would be justified. Nathaniel and Shackleton had accompanied them to the entrance to Devil's Canyon in case of further problems, but as there'd been none, they'd hurried on to meet their next assignment in Monotony.

Jim had then recruited Bryce's help. The sheriff hadn't needed any persuasion to lock up Albright, that attitude strengthening when Jim found that the evidence Albright had been determined would never be found was even more damning than he expected.

He had found a shallow grave near to Wilson's Crossing. Time had masked the exact cause of Narcissa's death, but in her death grip she'd gathered the best possible clue as to the identity of her murderer: Albright's tin star along with a torn scrap of his jacket.

Once that fact had been unearthed, the most likely explanation of events pointed to Narcissa coming to Wilson's Crossing to see Cooper. Albright had followed with some of the men he'd gathered around him.

An altercation had resulted in her death, but Mayor Maxwell, knowing of Narcissa's and Cooper's recent disagreement, had followed her. Albright had silenced him and later he'd killed the unfortunate Seymour Chambers and his daughter, but he'd not been able to finish the job with Cooper himself.

'Will you stay at Wilson's Crossing?' Jim asked.

'I will until Cooper's free, but after that . . . ' She cast him a sideways glance. 'I've not been good to you with my lying, but I'm grateful for what you did.'

'You hired me to find bones. That's what I did.'

'Then I hope that one day I come across some more.' She glanced up to Devil's Canyon. 'I can see the attraction of searching for them.'

She flashed him a smile, her face reddening in embarrassment, presumably because she was flirting while her brother was still in jail, so Jim didn't press the matter.

'The canyon looked to be a good place to search. I reckon I'll return one day to see what other interesting things I might find.'

She nodded. Jim clambered on to his wagon. He gave her a last cheery wave, then swung the wagon down the main road to head back to Carmon.

He'd telegraphed ahead and as his buyer would be expecting him within the week, he maintained a brisk speed. He expected to be waylaid, but he still kept to the most-travelled route alongside the creek.

Sure enough, he was five miles out of town when a familiar rider appeared on the trail ahead.

The man had stopped, as usual, at a point where the trail didn't allow a detour. This time he'd chosen a place where the creek was close on one side and the ground sloped steeply on the other.

Pierre Dulaine was alone, but Jim

had no doubt that other men would be lying in wait in the surrounding scrub.

'Monsieur Dulaine,' Jim hailed as he drew up, beaming a wide smile, 'I've been expecting you.'

'No distractions, Monsieur Dragon,' Pierre muttered. 'This time it'll be third time lucky.'

'If you were to best me, it'd be sixth time lucky, but I agree it's the third time we've met, and you've lost, this month.'

Pierre narrowed his eyes. 'Talk like that might force me to take your life as well as your cargo.'

'You wouldn't do that. You don't have the skill to find bones yourself, only to take them off the men who can. You need me.'

Pierre conceded this point with a shrug. 'Either way, this time I win. Your friends are heading to Monotony, so nobody can help you. There's just you, me, a load of hidden men with guns trained on you, and the bones in the back of your wagon. Best of all, this time I have enough time to check the whole wagon.'

'You do, but the first time the bones were hidden in the bottom of the wagon and the top was full of rocks. Then the bones were in the top and there was nothing hidden below.'

'They're the only two options. I win no matter which you've used.'

'Only two?' Jim leaned back. He moved to touch his lucky shark's tooth, then he drew his hand away and locked his hands behind his head. His smile grew. 'Do you want to search the wagon and then see if you can work out how I've fooled you this time. Or do you want to ride away without looking and with your dignity intact?'

Pierre's confident smile died.

THE END